THE ACCIDENTAL COUNTESS

ABOUT AN EARL BOOK 3

JESS MICHAELS

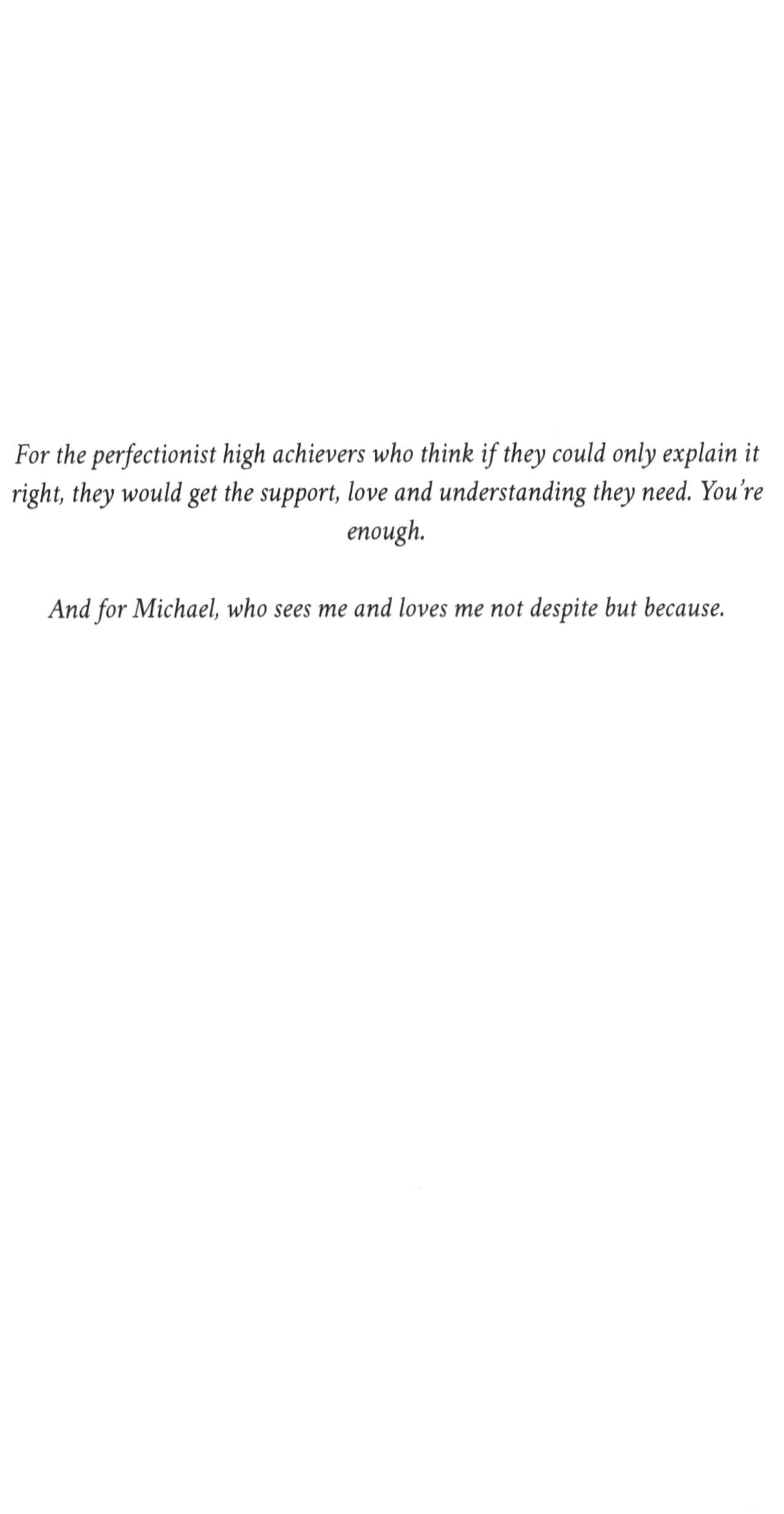

For the perfectionist high achievers who think if they could only explain it right, they would get the support, love and understanding they need. You're enough.

And for Michael, who sees me and loves me not despite but because.

CHAPTER 1

Unlike many rakes of his generation, Roderick Stratford, Earl of Kirkwood, actually believed in love. He had experienced it, after all, during the first fifteen years of his life, watching his besotted parents and their relationship, which often seemed to be plucked from the pages of a fairytale. It had created all his expectations of what his heart should feel for a future wife.

Their untimely deaths had shown him how deeply that same heart could break. But still, he believed, though he'd not yet found someone who engendered the tender feelings he required to wed.

"There you are! Having a brood, are we?"

Roderick stifled a laugh as he turned to face his old friend, Viscount George Lockhart. They'd been friends since school, thick as thieves, along with a handful of other young men, many of whom had taken their titles just as Roderick already had. Lockhart was still in waiting, though not with much anticipation, to come into his own earldom.

"A good brood is well-worth nursing," Roderick said as he extended a hand for a firm shake. "Especially while waiting for a friend to intrude. How are you, Lockhart? We kept missing each other all Season."

Lockhart rolled his eyes. "As you well know, Ramsbury and Delacourt both married recently, so my mother spent the last few months aiming me at every young woman from the current crop of debutantes. I hardly had time for any fun at all."

"And none caught your eye?" Roderick asked. "Made your heart flutter?"

Lockhart choked on a laugh. "You're the only one fool enough to think there's true love left in the world, friend."

"I beg to differ. The two earls you just mentioned have been very public about being in love with their wives."

"Ugh," Lockhart groaned. "Yes. I fear I shall be one of the last bastions of rationality in this cold, cruel world!"

"Well, at least the Season is coming to an end. I assume you'll go back to your estate in Derbyshire where you can hunt and carouse to your heart's content without interference?"

"That is the plan." His friend sighed. "But I have a *ghastly* duty to perform first."

Roderick smiled at the theatrical tone of Lockhart's voice. "And what is that?"

"Mama insists that I attend the party my aunt and uncle are holding over at their country home. She claims it's on my way to my estate, though it makes me go twenty miles away from my route and will be as exciting as watching toast brown." He stared at Roderick for a moment. "Why don't you come with me?"

Roderick couldn't help but laugh out loud. "After you just told me it was going to be boring and ghastly?"

Lockhart shook his head. "I was grousing, you know me. Not a serious bone in my body. It should be great fun."

"You are the worst liar." Roderick nudged him with his shoulder. "Why does your mother want you to go to this gathering?"

"Punishment for not finding a bride, first and foremost." Lockhart sighed. "But also because someone in our family must be represented at the gathering. You see, my aunt and uncle are trying to match my cousin, Miss Clarissa Lockhart."

Roderick wrinkled his brow as he tried to recall his friend's cousin. He could only find the brief image of a little girl with pigtails following Lockhart around when they were children. "I see. Was it her first Season?"

"No, her third." Lockhart shook his head. "She isn't quite a wallflower or a spinster yet, but I suppose that is the fear for the longer term. Hence the gathering where my aunt and uncle can better control who has access to her, and whether or not there are other eligible ladies in attendance to distract from her."

Roderick stared at him for a moment. "Are you trying to convince *me* to come to match with her?"

"You?" Lockhart snorted out a laugh. "Don't you worry. Not only would I never do that to you, I doubt you two would suit. Her obsession with propriety is legendary. She likely wouldn't look twice at a renowned rake like yourself. And you would be bored to the roots of your hair after ten minutes alone with her." He shook his head. "Don't mistake me, she's very kind and I adore her. But she'll settle for some meek little country mouse of a man who will follow her lead when it comes to every proper address, thought and action."

There was relief to that answer. Roderick hated it when ladies were thrown into his orbit. He truly believed that when he met the right one, it would hit him like a lightning bolt from above. He would know. *They* would know. One didn't find that from forced arrangements.

"I can see you are beginning to agree to my request," Lockhart said with a grin. "How about this—you come with me and spend a week and a half bearing a silly party, and then join me out at my estate for the real fun. We'll bed some willing women and run the dogs and horses ragged chasing game and drink too much."

Roderick shook his head with a laugh. "How could I deny you? Certainly, I'll join you if you'd like. Assuming it's agreeable to your aunt and uncle."

"Don't worry about that." Lockhart waved his hand dismissively. "I'll manage it. Then it's decided." He clapped Roderick on the shoulder. "Now what do you say we abandon this gathering and go somewhere the ladies are a bit more receptive, eh? I could use some London fun before I resign myself to country manners."

Roderick laughed as he followed his friend from the ballroom. Since he hadn't found his lady love this Season, he saw no reason not to continue to indulge in the kind of fun Lockhart meant. One couldn't be a reformed rake, after all, if one hadn't been a rake to start with. So he'd continue to revel in his dissipation at places like the Donville Masquerade and shadowy corners of Covent Gardens until he found a lady who tempted him from it.

And he didn't see that happening any time soon.

Miss Clarissa Lockhart was nervous as she paced her chamber, smoothing her white gown with her trembling hands, though she hadn't a wrinkle in the soft fabric.

"This will not do," she whispered to herself, and crossed to her bedside table. She snatched the book there and brought it to the fire where she could skim a few of the words better. Not that she needed to read them. She had pored over every word of this book, *The Mirror of the Graces*, since she had received it from her mother at the beginning of the Season. The pages of the etiquette manual were worn and dogeared from use, in fact.

"*Meek dignity,*" she read aloud. "*Chastened sportiveness and gentle seriousness.*"

She drew a deep breath and set the book down before she turned to look at herself in the mirror one final time. She was wearing just the right thing, at least according to her book, a muslin gown in white, just as all her gowns were. It was pretty, but not too showy. It was supposed to represent her goodness and virtue. Her hair was done properly, as well, in a demure yet pretty chignon at the base of her neck. Her cheeks, which she was careful to never let sun touch without protection, had been rouged, oh so very lightly, with carmine in its powdered form. Yes, she looked…oh, how did the book put it? *Wholesome*. Yes, she looked wholesome.

"There is nothing else I can do," she whispered to her reflection. She glanced at the clock on her mantel and sighed. It was time.

She left her chamber and took the winding route through the familiar halls of her childhood home. Over the years, she had watched the house become a little shabbier, though those things were covered up well enough for the gathering. It was up to her to raise the fortunes of her family. It always had been. She'd known that since she was twelve, almost a decade ago.

She reached the foyer and gave their longtime butler, Boulton, a smile. One she forced to fade more quickly than she might have once done. Her book had so many ideas on how friendly a lady should be to her servants, even ones she had adored since childhood.

"Your parents await you on the landing, Miss Lockhart," Boulton said with a swift incline of his head before he handed over her hat.

She sighed as she placed it on her head and tied it at her chin. In years past, she might have forgone the headwear and greeted her guests more simply, but the sun was not to be borne by ladies' skin, at least according to the author of her etiquette manual, so a hat it was.

She stepped outside and smiled at her parents. "Mama, Papa."

"The first carriage is arriving," her mother said with a nervous flutter to her hands. "Now, Clarissa, this is all for you, my dear. An opportunity I *know* you won't throw away after all we've done for you."

Clarissa drew in a deep breath as the weight of pressure came down on her shoulders and made her feel like she was sinking into the stone of the steps. "Yes, Mama. Of course, Mama."

Luckily, there was no more time for further advice or nerve-wracking observation from either of her parents, because the first carriage stopped along the drive and servants rushed forward to assist the guests.

Clarissa forced a serene smile to her lips for the gentleman who exited the carriage and reached back to help a lady do the same. It was

Viscount Crossworth and his mother. She felt a little relief at that, for at least the viscount was not ancient, nor entirely boring. Her mother and father had begun to shove her into the way of almost any eligible man around with a title or a fortune, regardless of disparate ages or situations. And though she had little choice but to honor their desires, she still hoped that whomever she matched with would be someone whose company she could bear for a lifetime.

The viscount had finished his greetings to her parents and stepped over to her. He had blonde hair and dark brown eyes that flitted over her face for a moment before he said, "Miss Lockhart. I'm so pleased to see you. I think the last time we met was at that garden fete mid-Season."

She nodded. "You've a good memory, my lord. I think you are exactly right. I'm so pleased you could join us."

"As am I. You recall my mother, yes?"

She spoke for a moment to Lady Crossworth, after which they entered the house to be escorted to their chambers. The guests arrived swiftly then, as if they'd all left London at the same time and caravanned their way to her doorstep. She greeted a marquess, this one older than her father, a few second sons with elevated positions, and another viscount before there was a lull in the arrivals.

She turned toward her parents. "You've found yourself quite the crop of eligible gentlemen for this gathering," she said carefully, trying not to offend even as she pressed her question. "Do we not worry that it will make it too obvious that you are on the hunt for a marriage for me?"

Her father shot her a side look. "Any lady worth her salt is always on the hunt for a marriage, Clarissa."

Her mother nodded. "At any rate, it won't all be gentlemen for you. Your cousin George will be here. And I invited the Earl and Countess of Ramsbury."

Clarissa's smile was more genuine now. "Oh, that's lovely. I saw them at the opera at the beginning of the Season and congratulated them on their marriage. I do enjoy the countess's company so much."

"And now that she isn't a spinster who could bring you down a peg, you can mine that friendship for the connections it could bring you," Mrs. Lockhart insisted with a pat of her hand.

Clarissa pursed her lips and turned her face away. How she hated the mercenary aspects of her parents' husband hunt. It had all grown all the worse in the last year, when Clarissa staggered into her third Season and they seemed to fear that meant she was failing.

Sometimes she felt the same, despite still being invited to every event and asked to dance by many gentlemen. Marriage was the only mark of success that mattered, and it was hard not to feel the sand of her life being pulled away, rushing her toward the next step when she would be bound to some man who would elevate her parents...and herself. Though *she* was an afterthought.

"And I think that is your cousin now," her mother said with a wave at the horses that were coming down the lane. "But who is with him?"

Clarissa lifted on her tiptoes to peer down the curve in the drive. Yes, it was George out front, she recognized her beloved cousin's gait on his mount, but the second man was not known to her. "Perhaps one of the other gentlemen, come from London on a horse rather than in a carriage?" she suggested.

But as they neared, Mrs. Lockhart lifted a hand to her chest. "Oh, that is the Earl of Kirkwood, I believe. I didn't think to invite him, myself. It's well known he isn't looking for a bride."

Clarissa wrinkled her brow. "You didn't invite him and yet he arrives with my cousin?" she repeated, and looked toward the rapidly approaching gentlemen again. "That is very rude, to come to a house party uninvited."

Certainly her handbook would have said so. She narrowed her gaze as the men grew ever closer.

"Well, he's rich and powerful," Mr. Lockhart said with a quick glare in her direction. "Imagine if you could land the unlandable! You were certainly raise all fortunes by doing so."

Clarissa pursed her lips as the men pulled their horses to a stop, each swung down and handed over the reins to waiting grooms. She examined the earl, especially. He was well-favored, of course. Tall, of lanky build and with dark hair that looked a little mussed from the road since he didn't wear a hat. His skin was slightly tanned, probably from the travel and when he looked up the stairs with a bored expression, she could not help but notice the finest dark green eyes she'd ever encountered. Ones that slid over her parents and then settled on her for a long moment before he had the audacity to wink at her as he followed her cousin up the stairs.

She huffed out a breath. Rich and powerful or not, this man already had two strikes against him for absolute rudeness. First to arrive without invitation and second to dare to engage himself with a lady he didn't even know.

"My dearest Uncle Marcus and Aunt Violet, I'm pleased to see you both," George said as he shook her father's hand and bussed her mother's cheek. "I hope you do not mind that I have come with a friend."

Clarissa saw Lord Kirkwood glance at George swiftly as her mother stepped forward. "Oh no, not at all! We're so pleased you have increased our party by one so lauded as the Earl of Kirkwood."

Kirkwood bent his head over her mother's hand as he lifted it to his lips. It was a showy act of chivalry, but it didn't ring entirely true. "I see my reputation proceeds me," he drawled. "Thank you for your hospitality, Mr. and Mrs. Lockhart. Your grounds are spectacular—I was admiring them as soon as we entered the estate."

"Couldn't stop waxing poetic about them," George agreed. Then he turned to Clarissa. "And there is the lady of the hour. Clarissa!"

Clarissa didn't have to force her smile for her cousin. He was a rapscallion, but she still adored him. Once upon a time her mother had thought she might be matched with him. After all he, too, would one day be an earl. Happily that notion had passed. George was more like a brother to her and he was wild as the day was long. A match would have been miserable.

"Dearest George," she said, and took his hand with both of hers. "You look a fright."

He laughed as he reached up to smooth his hair. "Do I? Well, that is only because I'm standing to one of the prettiest ladies in all the country."

Clarissa almost rolled her eyes, but then stopped herself. *The Mirror of the Graces* would never approve such behavior. Even less so in front of a stranger who was her better.

As if he sensed her thoughts about the earl, George turned toward him. "Have you had the pleasure of meeting my dear cousin, Kirkwood?"

"I haven't," the earl said, and stepped away from her mother. He smiled at her and she returned the expression with the smallest one of her own she could manage. She still thought this man abominably rude for inviting himself to a party and she couldn't let it go without some small consequence.

"The Earl of Kirkwood, I present Miss Clarissa Lockhart. My favorite cousin," George said.

Kirkwood reached out to take her hand and for a moment Clarissa thought he might lift it to his lips as he had done with her mother. Instead she shook it briefly and then withdrew. She thought his lips quirked a little in amusement, which she equally ignored.

"A pleasure to make your acquaintance, my lord," she said. "Though unexpected, indeed."

She saw her mother glare at her over the earl's shoulder and so she added a little curtsey to her comment out of respect to his rank. Mrs. Lockhart stepped forward. "George you will be in your usual chamber, and my lord, I'll give you the one just down the hall so you two friends may be close. Let me follow you in and tell our butler of the addition."

She motioned toward the door and George took her arm to lead her in. Kirkwood held Clarissa's stare a moment and then smiled. "I look forward to getting to know you better, Miss Lockhart. Good afternoon."

He followed her cousin and mother inside and Clarissa glared after them. When her father touched her arm, she jumped, for she hadn't realized he had moved closer as she focused on the departing party.

"You'll wrinkle if you look so cross," Mr. Lockhart said.

She bit back a little retort. One was to always receive advice from one's parents with deference, after all. Or so her book stated. She drew a breath. "Thank you, Father. You are likely correct. And I suppose if you and Mama aren't upset by the earl's unexpected arrival, then I shouldn't be either."

"No, not when he could be the best potential match here," her father said, and rubbed his hands together.

"But as Mama said when he approached, he doesn't seek a bride," Clarissa mused as she returned her attention to the drive and the next vehicle that was rumbling down the packed sand lane.

"By hook or by crook, every man of his rank must marry."

Clarissa glanced at her father. His eyes were lit up with plans. Even though the earl was a known rake, even though he would be so bold and uncouth. Even though surely a match between them could be nothing but dreadful. She could already tell they were polar opposites, more likely to be enemies than fall in love. Not that she expected love. Marriages were meant to be meetings of name and fortune, but she also hoped temperament and shared values.

But she didn't say any of that to her father. She couldn't because it would be going against what propriety demanded in a good daughter. And because she was interrupted by the next in a parade of gentlemen meant to be tempted by what she could bring to a union in her comportment and connection.

But the threat of matching with someone like the Earl of Kirkwood made her focus more fully on the matters at hand. She would just have to make herself even more tempting to the men who *did* align with her values in life. Then her parents couldn't be so foolish as to foist her off on someone frivolous and inappropriate. Handsome or not.

CHAPTER 2

Roderick strode down the hallway from the fine chamber where he had been placed and rapped on Lockhart's door, just one down from his own.

His heard his friend's voice from within. "Enter."

He did so and found Lockhart standing in the chamber, looking at the waistcoats he had brought with him. His valet held up one after another for George to examine.

"I'm glad you're here," Lockhart said with a brief glance at Roderick. "What do you think? The green or the blue?"

"The blue," Roderick said absently. "Did you not ask your aunt and uncle's leave in inviting me to join the party as we discussed?"

Lockhart pointed at the blue. "As the earl says, Jenkins. Have the rest pressed for supper tonight. You may go."

Jenkins swept up the items for his master's evening toilette and then bowed to Roderick before he left the room.

"Are you going to answer me?" Roderick pressed.

Lockhart wrinkled his brow. "You sound cross as the devil. What's got you in a twist?"

"My question," Roderick said and threw up his hands. "You invited me to join you and promised you would speak to your family about it. But your aunt and uncle seemed surprised to see me and your cousin was obviously irritated."

He couldn't help but briefly think of the lady with her fine features set just so on a slender face that matched her small frame perfectly. She had a simplicity to her appearance, but that only made her prettier. Except she had glared at him ever-so-slightly. She had spoken to him with an unmistakable chilliness to her tone.

"I told you that Clarissa was obsessed with propriety. And yes, it might have slipped my mind to request you join us."

Roderick thew up his hands. "Damn it, Lockhart."

"*But*," Lockhart continued, "my aunt and uncle were clearly over the moon to have so important a gentleman join the party. You saw them drooling all over you, I think my aunt nearly my lorded herself into an apoplexy. Although the Marquess of Mickenshire technically outranks you, he also has half your worth financially and when it comes to his connections. So you are, for all intents and purposes, the man of the highest importance to grace their halls."

Roderick stared. "That may be true, but it's meaningless. They've invited the others as potential suitors for your cousin, you said, but I'm certainly not that."

And that was true. Although he had noticed Miss Lockhart's finer qualities when it came to her beauty, he hadn't been struck by her in any other immediate way. There hadn't been any specific sparks when he took her hand. And she despised him, which wasn't what he anticipated when he met *the one*. So she *couldn't* be that, nor was she likely to be a lover to him, considering her virtue, her goals to marry well and her apparent dedication to all things proper.

All of which meant she was not of interest beyond polite conversation. That was the end of that.

"No. Poor girl." George shook his head. "Though some stuffy man with an acceptable rank will likely take her on, I fear she'll be miserable in the end."

"Yes, you've mentioned her obsession with proper manners several times. Out of curiosity, what brought that on?" Roderick asked.

George shrugged. "Likely the never-ending criticism of my aunt and uncle. The poor girl can never set a foot right, it seems, no matter what she does. And if anything doesn't go exactly as hoped, they all begin analyzing what she did to cause the problem." Now his friend looked truly troubled. "For her birthday just before the Season, my aunt gifted her a copy of *The Mirror of the Graces*."

Roderick shook his head. "I'm not familiar."

"Of course you aren't." George chuckled. "It's this ghastly etiquette manual designed to grind all the way into the ground every woman who buys in to its advice. I had a look at it during the fete we threw for Clarissa and couldn't get past the first bit when the author demanded the neckline be always covered or else a lady risked being seen as far too sensuous."

Roderick wrinkled his nose. "God help the entirety of Society, then, for current fashion dictates a lower neckline."

George shrugged. "And yet my cousin seems to have bought in to the entire scheme that if she only behaves with exact correctness she might solve all the problems for herself, her family and perhaps even the world."

Roderick frowned. He did not have any connection to the lady, but he did feel for her. "That's too bad, but I suppose there is nothing to be done about it. As you said, she'll likely match with some gentleman equally driven by such concerns and live her life very happily watching for every wrong turn of ankle or phrase."

"Indeed." George sighed. "At any rate, it seems you have forgiven me for failing to alert my aunt and uncle to your joining us."

"I suppose," Roderick said with a playful glare. "*If* you'll come with me for a walk around the garden. My legs are still stiff from the ride."

"I swear, you are like an old man," George said with a laugh. "Twenty-eight and already complaining of aches and pains. No, I won't today. I drank too much at the inn last night and I need to sleep so that I might be exceedingly dashing for the first supper of the party tonight."

Roderick shrugged. "Very well. Then I withhold my forgiveness. You'll have to make it up to me later. Rest well."

George's laughter followed him into the hall and Roderick was grinning as he made his way through the house, down the stairs and slowly through the winding passageways toward what he hoped would be an exit to the garden.

Most of the doors to the chambers were closed, but he peeked in at a few that were open. There was nothing particularly interesting in any of them, the usual small parlors and a music room. When he reached the end of the hall, however, he found a chamber that was almost entirely empty save for a worn-out chaise with a broken armrest and shabby fabric covering. The wallpaper here peeled at the water-damaged ceiling and there was a cracked pane of glass along the set of doors that led to the garden.

He frowned at the odd condition of the chamber, but stepped in nonetheless and crossed to exit outside. There was a small terrace with a set of stairs down and he took it with a breath of the fresh, warm air. The summer was coming to an end, but there was a still a softness to the breeze he'd always loved. Summer always made him feel younger, a bit more carefree.

He made his way through the garden, which was planted prettily with rosebushes which now had fading buds, tall trees whose leaves were just beginning to turn coppery and a few bushes that bore their end of season berries. There was nothing amazing about the space, but it was peaceful and comforting.

He strolled through the paths, pausing occasionally to look at a patinaed bronze fountain or smell the odd remaining flower. He was beginning to recover himself from the long ride when he glanced up and found he wasn't alone in the garden. There, across the way, standing beside a gazebo, was Miss Clarissa Lockhart. She still wore the hat with the large brim that shaded her face, but he recognized the white gown she'd worn earlier to greet her guests. The one he now noticed did indeed have a gauzy fabric tucked at the neckline to cover almost every inch of skin there. It seemed George was correct that she had taken the etiquette book to heart that his friend had described.

Roderick thought about turning away, avoiding the encounter, but at that moment she looked in his direction and he could see by the way her posture stiffened that she saw him. He sighed and started toward her.

"Miss Lockhart," he said. "I see we had the same idea to walk in the garden before preparing for supper."

Her lips pursed as he reached her, her brown eyes moving over him in an appraising fashion. She seemed to find his every fault, for her frown did not change.

"Lord Kirkwood. What a pleasure."

It didn't sound like a pleasure to her and Roderick stifled a smile at her pepper, which she was clearly trying to temper out of politeness. That little battle inside of her must have been exhausting.

"It's a wonderful garden," he said. "I am especially fond of that oak tree at the center."

They both turned toward the huge tree with its thick trunk and wide branches that provided shade to a good portion of the garden.

"It has been here since even before the house, my lord," she said. "They estimate it to be over three hundred years old."

He nodded and didn't have to pretend to be impressed. "It has seen a great deal of change then. Had many a youth climb it, perhaps even a few young lovers carve their initials in its bark."

Her gaze held his a moment and then flitted away. "I'm sure."

"You've never looked?" he asked with a laugh as he stepped toward the tree. He slowly moved around it, looking up the length as far as he could manage. He had almost completed the turn when he saw, high up, the faint scar of a heart. "There!"

She had been standing back, but now she rushed forward to join him and looked up where he pointed.

"Oh, you're right," she said, the coldness removed from her tone for a moment. "What initials are they there?"

He squinted. "It looks like an AR and a FL or maybe a PL?"

She made a soft sound from her throat and he turned to see her gazing at the heart. "I wonder why I never noticed it."

"Well, it's at least three feet above my head," he said. "And you're a head shorter than I am. Anyway, sometimes we don't see what's right in front of us."

"I suppose that's true," she mused and then she turned her gaze on him. Her lips thinned once more, whatever little truce she'd allowed when they examined the oak tree gone. "Well, I should go in. Please enjoy your walk, my lord."

"I will," he said with a slight bow. "I look forward to speaking with you more later."

She didn't respond to that, but gave a small curtsey and headed back toward the house. She moved to a larger set of stairs that went to the main terrace above and disappeared from his view once the angle became too high.

It was plain the woman didn't like him and he supposed it didn't bother him. Or at least it shouldn't. So he shrugged it off and continued his turn about the garden, at peace with the fact that the oh-so-proper Miss Lockhart was not someone he would have to concern himself with.

Although the gathering at her family's estate was meant to be a way to present her to eligible suitors, Clarissa couldn't help but feel a burst of relief when she discovered one of the people seated next to her at supper was Lady Ramsbury. She'd known Marianne before her marriage, though hadn't been allowed much to interact since the countess had once been a wallflower. A failure, Mr. and Mrs. Lockhart had said, implying, of course, that Clarissa could easily follow in those footsteps if she wasn't careful.

But now Marianne was a welcomed addition, an encouraged

connection, because she had at last married well and was in a position of power.

"You do look lovely in that blue, my lady," Clarissa said, looking with longing at the silk of her friend's gown. It was so fine, in an icy blue with short puffed sleeves and cords of the same fabric coming down across the bodice. Even though Marianne's collarbones were revealed, it didn't seem immodest.

And yet, Clarissa knew she couldn't be so bold. Etiquette said that a young lady should not be too showy, and exhibit her modesty and innocence by wearing only white gowns.

"Thank you," Lady Ramsbury said with a genuine smile. "Sebastian picked out the fabric himself. I love it, for it matches his eyes."

They both glanced down the table where the earl was sitting near her cousin, George. The two men had known each other a long time and were talking in a friendly manner. Lord Ramsbury seemed to sense his wife's regard, though, for he turned those startling blue eyes toward her, smiled with a heavy dose of wickedness and lifted his glass as if to toast her.

Clarissa broke her gaze away from the inappropriate show of their connection, but Lady Ramsbury only laughed. "I swear, the man delights in reminding all that he might be a very reformed rake, but a rake he most definitely once was."

Clarissa shifted. The idea of a rake put her to mind of a different earl. Lord Kirkwood and his playful demeanor in the garden earlier. He'd acted as if he wasn't doing something wrong by being here and engaged her in conversation without thought to their lack of relationship. If that was what one got with a rake, she was not interested. The man was, of course, terribly handsome, but so were a great many men. Looks weren't everything.

"I'm very happy for your joy, my lady," Clarissa said. "And that you could join us at this gathering. I've always wished to better make your acquaintance."

Lady Ramsbury smiled at her. "As have I. I think you and I might have a great deal in common. You are of a bookish sort, yes?"

Clarissa winced. Indeed, she had always loved to read and study up on every subject she could find. As a young girl, her parents hadn't seemed to care enough to put her love of learning to a stop. But after her first Season out when she hadn't landed a husband, they'd begun to intervene. Imply that she might be viewed as a bluestocking and seen as less desirable if she were too clever.

"I-I fear I have little time for books anymore," she said.

Lady Ramsbury's brow knitted as if she didn't fully understand that idea. "Well, if you are of a mind, Sebastian and I finished up a very good novel on our way from London. I'd be happy to lend it to you."

"You and the earl...read together?" Clarissa asked, looking again at Ramsbury at the other end of the table. He was laughing at something one of his companions said.

"Oh, yes," Lady Ramsbury replied. "He's always been a great reader and enjoys sharing a story with me, or deeper fare where we can discuss history or even politics."

Clarissa pursed her lips. The idea of finding a mate who might actually celebrate her mind was a bewitching one. And yet that wasn't the way she classified the men she encountered in her search for a husband. Compatibility had more to do with rank and influence and steering away from anyone she didn't think she could stand for the rest of her life.

"That's lovely," she said.

Lady Ramsbury looked at her a moment, then changed the subject. They began to talk of the recently ended Season and Clarissa relaxed at the more benign topic. Sometimes when she was forced to face her husband hunt, there was a flare of panic in her chest. A true terror. But she couldn't afford that.

Soon enough the supper ended and the men separated from the women to have their port and a game of billiards. The women began to make their way toward the parlor where the group would reconvene later to play some games and talk. Clarissa saw that her mother was waiting for her to help lead the group and hustled to walk with her.

"You spoke with Lady Ramsbury for a long time during supper," Mrs. Lockhart said without much preamble.

Clarissa nodded. "Yes, I was so pleased to get a chance to reconnect with her and—"

"But you all but ignored the marquess. He was seated on your right," her mother interrupted.

Clarissa bit her tongue so she would not reply too sharply or swiftly. Respect for one's parents. She had to recall that. "I suppose I didn't," she agreed. "He is...he's much older than I am, you know. I think he fell asleep during supper."

They entered the parlor and her mother faced her. "What does his age matter? He's a fine prospect, for his late wife only gave him daughters and he wants a son, which you could provide."

Clarissa gasped at such an uncouth suggestion. "Mama, please lower your voice."

Mrs. Lockhart glared at her but did so. "And he is finely situated. He could definitely help right things for your father and I."

Clarissa didn't respond. How could she? This was the constant conversation, after all. The constant desperate stir that her mother created when the topic came up. "Yes, Mama."

Her mother shook her head. "If you don't like him, then there are others, you know. Even your cousin has provided us with a fine and unexpected opportunity by bringing the Earl of Kirkwood. He's certainly young enough for your lofty standards and no one could say he isn't handsome."

Clarissa stepped back. "We wouldn't suit."

Mrs. Lockhart shook her head and a great sadness entered her gaze. "You would be so selfish, would you? You would deny your parents?"

She tsked and then walked away to some of the other women, leaving Clarissa to watch after her with a heavy heart. Despite all her attempts to be open to the needs and wants of her parents, despite trying to honor and respect them, the fact that neither of them seemed to count her happiness when they thought of her future was...

Painful. It was painful. But it was also a fact of life. And so she pushed the emotion away and she hoped cleared it from her expression before she stepped up to speak to some of the other ladies in attendance. The way to end the interference in her life was to simply do what her family required.

And that was to find the right husband as swiftly as possible. Before either of them decided to take matters into their own hands.

CHAPTER 3

Roderick always forgot how utterly tedious a country party could be until he was trapped in the midst of one. And now, three days after his arrival to Mr. and Mrs. Lockhart's, he found himself nearly going out of his skull with boredom as he stood over the sideboard, looking at what was left in the selection of breakfast.

Oh, he had friends here. Lockhart and Ramsbury were great fun, though Ramsbury now sequestered himself with his wife more often than not. They were in love. Head over heels. Roderick couldn't begrudge his friend that, as it was exactly what he, himself, sought.

As if conjured by the thought, Ramsbury entered the breakfast room, his hair a little mussed and his eyes slightly bleary despite the late hour.

"Kirkwood," he said with a good-natured slap on the shoulder. "You're up early."

"It's eleven," Roderick laughed as he handed over a plate and stepped aside so they could look at the spread together. "I think we might be the last ones."

"Hmmm," Ramsbury murmured with a little smirk. "Well, some days it is harder to get out of bed than others."

"I imagine so in your current position as a besotted husband."

Something softened in his old friend's expression. "It will be the position I hold for the rest of my life."

"Then I'm truly happy for you," Roderick said. "You and the countess do seem well suited, so I suppose that what they say is true."

"They?" Ramsbury put a few items on his plate. "What do *they* say?"

"Something about reformed rakes and the best husbands."

Ramsbury laughed. "True only if one is in love with one's wife. Which I am. And now I shall rejoin the lady, herself, and deliver sustenance to tempt her back to the party. But I hear there will be some lawn games before tea to get the blood pumping to prepare for the ball tonight. I look forward to trouncing you soundly at pall-mall."

He gave a little salute and then swept from the room, apparently back to his waiting wife. Roderick's smile fell. There was the proof, yet again, of true love out there in the world. But *he'd* never even come close. Every one of his many lovers had been transactional, a pleasant way to purge a physical desire. He had never felt drawn enough to any woman that he would officially court her.

He shook his head. He was young still, with plenty of time to be struck by the lightning he knew would accompany meeting his future love. In the meantime, he would continue to enjoy his life. Starting with a spirited game of pall-mall.

Clarissa tried to school her expression as she stood to the side of the pall-mall court and watched the play, her mallet gripped in her hand. They had a large enough party that they had split into two groups, declaring that the winners amongst them would face each other in the end for the ultimate prize. Normally she would have enjoyed the match, her group was to go second and to display herself with chastened sportiveness was one of the required abilities of *The Mirror of the Graces*.

If she were honest, it was one she struggled with. How was she to display both playfulness *and* restraint? To be both quiet *and* enthusiastic? It was one of the many parts of her handbook that she read over and over and tried to define for herself so that she wouldn't fail.

Right now trying to display both was even harder because one of the gentlemen on the field of play was Lord Kirkwood. He was with Lord Ramsbury; Mr. Longford, who was a second son; Clarissa's mother; and Lord Crossworth's mother. Kirkwood was laughing loudly, drawing attention to himself. And he had stripped from his jacket and rolled his sleeves to the elbows in a shocking display of dishabille. Even his dark hair was a little mussed because between shots down the alley, he kept running his fingers through it.

It all felt entirely ungentlemanly and uncouth. Everyone was meant to pay attention to their grooming, to be modest in their attire. To do otherwise displayed a familiarity that couldn't be born.

Not to mention, his forearms were distracting. Lined with lean muscle, peppered with light brown hair, there was just too much skin there. She could see others had noticed. Mr. Longford's sister, Beatrice Vale, for example, couldn't seem to *stop* staring, despite being in her late thirties and a relatively recent widow. Surely she should have more decorum.

"Ah!" Kirkwood crowed, drawing her attention back as his ball rolled through the raised ring at the end of the alley in, she had to admit, an impressive shot. It had to be at least twenty-five feet from where he had started.

"I would accuse you of cheating, but I cannot determine how," Ramsbury said with a chuckle as he reached out to shake Kirkwood's hand. "But I'll give Marianne as much advice as I can so that she will beat you after she wins the next round."

"I'm terrible at pall-mall, dearest," Lady Ramsbury declared as she slid her hand through Clarissa's arm and they walked onto the alley together as the servants gathered up the balls to return them to the opposite end. "I fear I shall not redeem the honor of our title."

The whole party was laughing now and Clarissa joined in. Somehow Ramsbury or Marianne being playful didn't bother her as much as Kirkwood doing it. She stepped past him with only the slightest look, though she heard him give a little snort of laughter.

"Lady Ramsbury, I believe you have the rank and thus the first shot," George said as the players aligned themselves.

Marianne lined up her shot and swung her mallet, but it turned out she was just as hopeless at the game as she had declared, for she hardly rolled the ball forward and also slid it to the very edge of the alley.

"You see," she called back with a little smile for her husband.

He looked anything but annoyed by her failure and Clarissa found her smile falling. If *she* missed her shot, she would hear no end of it from her father, who chose not to play, but was obviously judging all who did.

"Are you quite well, Miss Lockhart?" Lord Crossworth asked. "Your face is suddenly pinched."

She almost gasped in horror that she had been seen as such. Showing such dark emotions was not done, certainly not in public. Rarely in private. "Oh, I apologize. I was just thinking about..." She glanced at Lord Kirkwood and found him watching her closely. "Thinking about my best strategy for a shot. Perhaps you could advise?"

She didn't need the advice, of course. But this was what women did. They pretended to be less so that men could act like more. An annoyance, but also an expectation she was bound to uphold if she wanted to follow societal rules.

Lord Crossworth began to talk and she mostly blocked him out, just nodding and murmuring little sounds of affirmation. Instead, she was still distracted by Kirkwood. He arched a brow at her and then he had the audacity to wink. He winked at her! She, an unmarried miss. He a...a rogue...a scoundrel. A rake!

She took a long step away from the viscount, hardly realizing that he was still talking, and strode up to her ball. With a grunt she swung the mallet and hit the ball so hard that it soared upward as well as forward and landed with a thud far farther than anyone else's had.

She wanted to shout with the achievement, but managed to keep her wits and her composure. As the rest of the crowd clapped she gave one last glare toward Kirkwood and made her way down the alley.

They continued the game that way, taking their turns one after the other. Poor Marianne never fully recovered from her bad first hit, but she laughed with real pleasure at the game each time. In the end, it came down to Clarissa and Lord Crossworth. He lined up for his shot, his face increasingly serious about the endeavor. When he swung the mallet, the ball rolled forward and then stopped just next to the ring. His lips pinched with obvious frustration before he turned toward Clarissa.

"Your shot, Miss Lockhart," he said with an indulgent smile that only served to irritate her further. "May I advise you so that you get as close to the ring as possible?"

"No, thank you, my lord. I believe I can manage," she said.

She heard her mother make a little noise from the crowd. Wonderful, it seemed she had done something else wrong. Refused the assistance of a potential suitor, in front of others. Forget that she had been playing better than he had for the entire round.

But now she was in a pickle. She knew she could make the shot before her. It was long, but she had a good angle. If she did so, though, that meant besting Crossworth. She wasn't supposed to do that. Etiquette said that a lady was to defer to a man. Especially one she might link herself to.

And yet, if she won, she would face Lord Kirkwood in the final round. There would be such pleasure in defeating *him*, if only to take the smug satisfaction from his handsome face. To show him that poor manners could not be rewarded.

She drew a long breath, swung her mallet and hit it just so. The ball rolled and she leaned forward, feeling all in the crowd do the same. It began to slow as it approached the ring and Lord Crossworth smiled.

"No shame in—" He cut himself off as the ball cleared the ring and the crowd behind her erupted in applause and shouts of support.

Crossworth turned toward her, a smile on his face that did not reach his eyes. He held out a hand. "Good show, Miss Lockhart."

"You are too kind. It was purely luck," she lied. "And your good advice."

She took his hand and he shook it, but he squeezed as he did so, a little too hard to be friendly. She pulled her hand away and rubbed it slightly as he turned from her and went to accept the condolences of the other gentlemen.

"It will be Clarissa and Kirkwood to the death, it seems!" George crowed. "I'll be taking wagers to the side if anyone would like to partake."

He was teasing and Clarissa laughed, but many of the gentlemen actually approached him. She shook her head. Men could be ridiculous on what they wagered on.

As the servants gathered up the balls and retrieved mallets from the other players, Clarissa made her way back down the alley. Her father stepped in as she did so, his long face even longer with a scowl.

"Why did you defeat the viscount?" he whispered.

She glanced at him. "It was a friendly game, Father. I merely had the luck of it."

He glowered at her. "I have spared no expense to bring these men here for you to exhibit without competition. Do not make me regret it. When you face off with Lord Kirkwood, don't repeat this foolishness. He is even more important than Crossworth and could raise you higher if you don't muck it up as you've done so many times before."

"You cannot possibly wish for me to match with—"

But she couldn't finish the sentence. Her father moved away from her and she sighed, letting her shoulders roll forward. She should have guessed her parents would see Kirkwood as a mighty catch, despite how ill-suited he would be to her. That didn't matter to them. It was not supposed to matter to her.

"Deference to one's parents," she murmured as a reminder to herself. She didn't have to fear. Kirkwood couldn't possibly want her. And if she behaved correctly, she might catch the eye of some other gentleman and that would end their interest. Not Crossworth, it seemed, for he still glared at her.

But there were others here who would watch her match with Kirkwood. So she would have to be demure. Meek. And let Kirkwood win, just as her father suggested.

"That was an excellent show, Miss Lockhart," Kirkwood said as he stepped up to her at the end of the alley. "I was mightily impressed by your final shot."

She looked up at him. He seemed genuine in the compliment. Probably trying to soften her up for the battle to come. No, not a battle. She was letting him win, after all.

"I certainly cannot compare to you," she choked out.

His brow wrinkled and he opened his mouth, but the footman arrived with their balls for the game and the crowd gathered closer.

"You have the rank, my lord," she said, inclining her head.

"A gentleman always defers to the lady," he replied. "Please."

She narrowed her eyes at him. He wanted her to go first. Out of politeness or because he wanted to see her shots to know what he needed to do. A good strategy, honestly, but one that irritated her once more when it came to him.

"Thank you," she managed to choke out with a false smile. "How kind."

He made that little sound in the back of his throat again, almost a chuckle that she doubted anyone else could hear. She stepped up to the line at the beginning of the alley, set her ball down and drew a breath. Let him win.

She knocked the ball with the mallet and it rolled forward with just half the strength that she had used in the prior game. There was polite applause as she stepped aside and Kirkwood took his place on the line. He shot her an odd look, then swung his mallet and hit the ball with a crack. It rolled and she frowned as it stopped just barely farther than her own.

They moved forward together, the crowd on either side of the alley doing the same. "You can best him, Clarissa!" Marianne called from the side with a wide smile. "Do it for the honor of the ladies!"

Clarissa returned the smile even though her stomach felt sick. What she wanted to do was wallop the ball as hard as she could and take this man in the least number of shots possible. To make him sweat when he realized he couldn't win against her, a lady. Take him down a peg or two and then accept the congratulations of the women in attendance while the men had to pay their wagers out because they hadn't believed she could win.

"Deference to one's parents," she murmured under her breath.

Kirkwood tilted his head. "What was that?"

She ignored him and hit the ball. She hit it harder this time, but purposefully drove it off the best line, resulting in an "awwww" from the gathered crowd.

"Oh no," she said, trying to put as much genuine disappointment in her tone when she was actually impressed with herself that she could purposefully put the ball exactly where she wished to.

"Indeed." Kirkwood's tone was dry and he stepped up, met her gaze, and without looking, hit the ball. It rolled forward and also to the side, nearly hitting hers.

She glared at him. Was he doing that on purpose? Matching her shot for shot? Why would he do that?

She gave him a sickly-sweet smile. "We seem to be well matched, my lord."

He arched a brow. "Don't we just? I wonder at it, for we both seemed to perform better in the previous rounds."

She huffed out a breath. And now he was drawing attention to their mutual bad play? The man had no sense of decorum at all. A gentleman would have ignored it, played his round and then been chivalrous about her loss. Why could he not follow even those most basic rules of courtship?

No, not courtship. She shook her head at that thought. Interaction. That was what she'd meant. She was just all turned around in her head thanks to the potential suitors all around.

"Are you going to play, Miss Lockhart?"

She blinked. "I-I was just thinking about my strategy to get out of this awful angle."

"Ah." He didn't look like he believed her and made no attempt to cover that expression. "Yes. We've both gotten ourselves into quite the predicament."

She forced her countenance to remain calm and aligned her mallet before she swung and sent the ball rolling. Oh, she had hit it too hard in her frustration and this time it rolled into the middle of the alley and within a shot's length of the ring. Drat and damn. If he continued to play poorly, whether by design or accident, she would be hard pressed to win.

He flashed her a smile as he aligned and took his shot. Like her, he hit better and his ball rolled close to hers. He was definitely doing this on purpose.

"Hmmm," she murmured as they walked up together. "It seems our fortunes are bound. I wonder why that is?"

He shrugged one shoulder. "A question for the ages. It seems you'll win here, Miss Lockhart, as you are within a shot of the ring."

She pursed her lips. She was determined to do as her father had asked. Or at least, that was what she tried to tell herself. In truth, now she wanted Kirkwood to win because somehow *that* had become how she would beat him. But she had to be careful. She couldn't be too obvious. The crowd, when she actually noticed it was there in her focus on the earl, was already murmuring and putting their heads together to discuss this odd round.

She worried her lip a little and looked over to find him watching her. He tilted his head almost as if to say, *Well?*

She scowled and hit the ball. It rolled forward, slid a little off-line and stopped within a tap's distance of the ring.

His smile fell and he stared at her. "I see," he said softly.

"Yes. It's bad luck, isn't it?" She made her voice as sweet as she could. "Ugh, so frustrating. It looks to be your game, my lord."

"It does." He hit the ball and it rolled forward, passing hers slightly, but not making it into the ring. "Ah, curses."

"Curses?" she repeated under her breath as she shot him a look.

He smiled. She almost wanted to stomp her foot in frustration, all reminders that all things must be in moderation for ladies, especially emotions, forgotten because of the irritating person at her side.

But she drew a few breaths and looked at her options. There was almost no way not to win here. Her shot was too close to pretend she had gone off unless she faked an injury and that was going too far. Unless…

She smiled as the solution formed in her head. It would take a little talent, but she'd always been good at pall-mall. She drew in a long breath, exhaled and hit her ball. It rolled toward the ring, then slightly to the side, struck Kirkwood's ball and slid it into the ring instead of her own.

"Oh!" George called out, startling her as she had forgotten, once again, about the crowd watching in suspense. "Kirkwood wins due to Clarissa's pushing him into the ring!"

There was applause from the crowd and Clarissa found herself grinning as Kirkwood stared at his ball on the other side of the ring. When he looked at her, though, the grin faded. He tilted his head. "Good show, Miss Lockhart."

"What do you mean, my lord?" she asked as she extended her hand in congratulations. "You took the day."

He took her hand and his thumb grazed across her skin briefly. "Did I?"

The others rushed in to congratulate him and console her before the group of them started back up toward the house for refreshments and then to separate to prepare for the ball that night. Kirkwood was pushed forward by the men, who were clearly celebrating whether he'd won the day by her move or his own. He smiled slightly but when he looked back over his shoulder at her, her heart beat a little faster. He arched a brow and then winked. Like he knew what she'd done.

Just as she knew what he'd been doing. She scowled.

"Oh, don't feel badly," Beatrice Vale said, mistaking her frown for disappointment. "The earl is such a good player."

Clarissa shot her a look. "Yes," she ground out.

"And he cuts a fine figure," Beatrice continued, and all but batted her eyes at his retreating figure.

Why Clarissa was so annoyed by that, she couldn't say. The widow could have him. Certainly she didn't want him for herself. The Earl of Kirkwood could hang for all she cared. His good looks weren't enough to tempt her. They never would be.

CHAPTER 4

Roderick stood at the edge of the ballroom, couples bobbing by him in dance after dance, and yet he hardly noticed them. His mind kept going back to hours ago on the pall-mall court. To the bright triumph on Clarissa Lockhart's face when she had…well, she'd let him win. *Forced* him to win, if he was clear about it, entirely against his will. Why, he had no idea. It had become a battle between them, just as everything had felt like a battle with the woman since his arrival.

He glanced across the room and found her chatting with a group of women. Sometimes she would grow excited and her hands would begin to move in animated display, but she'd catch herself and immediately temper the action, bending her head. Returning to the demure exhibition she seemed to think was required in company.

It was all an act, just like her losing to him was an act. She was always pretending, it seemed. Only her dislike of Roderick appeared to be genuine, which was both infuriating and fascinating. And perhaps it was time to resolve all that at last so he could stop thinking about it.

He moved across the room just as the other ladies left her. She turned toward him and the smile fell from her face. She corrected herself quickly enough, becoming blank and serene, but he'd seen it. He would almost laugh at it, but there was some strange drive within him to understand it. Perhaps because she was the cousin of a good friend.

"Miss Lockhart, a pleasure to meet you again when we are not on the battlefield."

She sniffed rather than laughed. "It was hardly a battle, my lord. I was routed."

He arched a brow. "That isn't exactly how I recall it, but I would never correct you."

Her lips thinned a little, but she made no retort even if he sensed one on her tongue. "Are you enjoying yourself?" she asked.

He nodded. "Yes. A great deal. Many of the attending parties are friends or at least good companions. And those invited to the ball from the surrounding area have increased the pleasure of the night. This is a triumph for you and your parents."

Her brows knitted together, as if she hadn't expected that response. Didn't trust it, it seemed. But she was thrown off and he had to believe this was the best time to...*strike* was the word that came to mind. As if they were still engaged in mental combat on the pall-mall field.

"Would you do me the honor of dancing the next with me?"

The color left her cheeks and she hesitated. He could see she wished to reject him. It was almost comical. But then she inclined her head. "I could not refuse."

"Of course you could," he said.

Her gaze darted to the dancefloor. He realized then what the problem was. Propriety dictated that if she refused one partner, she was required to keep herself from the dancefloor for the rest of the night. He hadn't meant to trap her like that and he took a step back with his hands slightly raised.

"I would retract the offer if you truly didn't wish it, and say nothing about it so that you might continue your evening."

She jerked her gaze to his and he caught his breath. Hidden within the dark brown of her stare was a little green. He hadn't noticed it before, but it made her eyes so very different from any other lady's.

"That is a chivalrous offer, but to do so would be dreadfully rude on my part. I-I would be happy to dance with you, my lord," she said a little more softly both in volume and tone. She extended a hand and he took it to guide her to the dancefloor.

It was a waltz. He hadn't intended that. It felt a little too close and intimate to perform with a woman who did not like him, nor wish to be near him, let alone fully in his arms. But it was too late now to change things. She placed a hand on his shoulder, another in his and he lightly touched her hip. They turned out together for a while, though she kept her gaze on a spot that wasn't exactly his face.

"I have never been to this part of Leicestershire before," he said, trying to find a benign topic to soften Miss Lockhart before he tried to determine the source of her dislike. "It's lovely."

"It is," she agreed.

He waited for her to expound, but she didn't and he sighed as they turned a few more times in silence. "Do you have any recommendations for things to do during my visit?"

She pursed her lips and then said, "The Duke and Duchess of Rutland are in the midst of building a new Belvoir Castle on the site of the old ruin. It's far from finished, but the grounds are lovely. You might even get permission to fish in one of the lakes, if you're of a mind. My cousin could arrange it, I'm sure."

They pivoted to the beat of the music, which he could tell was coming to its end. "Ah yes, Rutland. He breeds fine thoroughbreds, as well."

"He's known for that, yes." The music faded at last and she stepped back to give him a deep curtsey. Her expression seemed more relaxed now and she glanced away from him, like she was counting the moments until they were parted. "Thank you, Lord Kirkwood."

He took her hand to escort her from the floor. They stopped to the side and he tilted his head to look at her more closely. "I do not think you like me much, Miss Lockhart."

Her lips parted and he could see he had startled her. "That is very direct."

"I find it is easier when one is. I note you do not deny it."

"Because it is also an entirely impertinent observation to make of someone you hardly know. Very rude." The words bubbled from her lips and she paled instantly. She shifted and then said, "Forgive me. I should not have said that."

"Why-ever not? I prefer it, for it's far more honest than glaring daggers at me across every room I enter. So, you believe me rude."

She shoved her hands down at her sides and drew a long breath before she curtseyed to him a second time. "Please excuse me."

She pivoted and walked away and he watched her with increasing frustration. The woman was impossible. He should have let her go, simply walked away with a shrug at her strenuous dislike and rigid idea of proper comportment and find something more entertaining to do. Mr. Longford's sister, Mrs. Vale, had been making eyes at him all day. She was a widow—if she was open to it, he could have a bit of fun at least. That would make him forget the entirely unpleasant, if lovely, Miss Lockhart.

And yet he didn't filter back into the crowd and find the lady who actually seemed to *want* to spend time with him. Instead, he followed the one who made it increasingly clear she didn't. Through the crowd, out the terrace door and around to a quiet corner of the wide veranda. She had stopped at the terrace wall and gripped her hands into fists against the rough stone there as she looked out onto the moonlit garden.

"Miss Lockhart," he said.

She turned to face him. "Gracious, why must you continue to harangue me?"

Her cheeks were pink with angry color and her eyes snapped with the same. It made her even prettier and more interesting to look at. But he ignored that and folded his arms.

"Because *you* are adept at avoiding a simple, straightforward conversation. You dislike me. Greatly, it seems, though I don't think we've ever had the displeasure of encountering each other before I dismounted from my horse on your drive not four full days ago. So unless we have some shared history I've forgotten, then I can only assume all this vitriol you are barely containing is about me committing the cardinal sin of arriving to your family home uninvited? Is that why?"

She seemed to struggle with a response, but at last she folded her arms and took a long step toward him.

"*Yes*," she snapped out. "I find the fact that you have intruded uninvited into a party of a family you do not know is *abominably* rude and entitled. Are you happy now, Kirkwood? May I be freed from this ridiculous interrogation?"

The words spilled from her mouth, laced with all the anger she so often repressed down deep in her chest, and Clarissa immediately wished she could take them back. Just as she had in the ballroom a few moments before and earlier on the pall-mall alley, she was allowing her emotions take over. According to etiquette guides, that was one of the deepest sins a lady could commit. And yet this man, this tall and handsome and really entirely annoying man, seemed to bring them out. That was the very best reason to avoid him if he would ever let her do so.

"Please," she said, drawing a few breaths. "Forgive my lapse in manners and let me go."

He caught her hand instead of doing so and she stiffened. He'd touched her during the dance, as well, and she felt an odd reaction through her body when he did. Not entirely unpleasant, though certainly foreign. Was it disgust? No, it didn't feel like that. It was like warmth that spread through her. What did one call such a thing that no other gentleman had ever inspired?

"I asked you for the truth of your feelings," he said, his tone making it clear that he was only clinging to control just as she was.

"So you needn't apologize. But you must allow me to respond to your charge."

She shook his hand away and folded hers in front of herself, willing them to stop tingling. She didn't want to let him respond. She wanted him to bow his head and just go away so his presence would stop troubling her so much.

But that wasn't fair, was it? Certainly this entire situation made her just as impolite as she wanted to believe him. She let out a shaky sigh. "Yes. I suppose I owe you that."

He ran a hand through his hair, disrupting the smooth lines of the style and making him look as rakish as he was rumored to be. "I've been mates with your cousin George for years, you know. And so when he approached me in London at the end of the Season and asked me to accompany him to his estate, with a stop here at your gathering, I agreed."

She sucked in a breath to retort, but he held up a hand and it stopped her, as annoyed as she was by the act.

"*But*," he continued with a little glare. "I also insisted he ensure that my presence would be expected and welcome by your family. He agreed and since he said nothing to the contrary before our departure, I assumed it was until I dismounted Othello and found everyone in your family either shocked or annoyed to see me there."

Her anger cooled a little at that entirely understandable and rational explanation. "Oh."

He arched a brow at her tiny response. "So, yes, I agree that it is *very* rude to come uninvited to a gathering with a family I hardly know. And yet, that was not my intent, even if it was the result of circumstances out of my control."

She stared at him a moment, lit by the moon and the glittering candlelight of the ball through the windows. He looked truly bothered by this conversation. She had no idea if that was real, but she had no reason to doubt him. Or at least none she could find when she didn't even know him.

"I-I could see how my cousin might do such a thing," she admitted at last. "He is a dear little rapscallion at best. And a forgetful clod at worst."

"He is, indeed, often both those things at once," Kirkwood agreed with a half grin that made him even more attractive. She wanted to return it with a smile of her own, but forced her expression to remain unmoved.

"Is—is your horse really named Othello?" she asked.

He seemed surprised by the question, but he nodded. "He is. A favorite Shakespeare play of mine."

She shifted her weight with discomfort. She would also count Othello amongst her favorite plays from the Bard. Having that in common with this man was a bit...infuriating.

"Miss Lockhart, would you like me to leave?" he asked. "Depart your home now that we understand each other? If my presence is that difficult for you to bear, despite my explanation, I could find a reason to depart that would leave you with none of the blame. It's your home, after all, and despite what you seem to think of me, I wouldn't want to leave you in discomfort in your own walls."

She worried her lip. For the second time, she found him being chivalrous, trying to think of her comfort. First when he had told her he wouldn't hold her to a dance if she didn't wish it. And now. Of course whether he was here or not, she would not feel comfortable in her own walls. She didn't think she ever truly had. She shoved those thoughts aside, refusing to ponder them.

"No. I've been unfair to you, I think," she said softly. "Which was as vulgar of me as I accused you of being without all the facts. Perhaps we can forgive each other and start over."

"I'd like that," he said.

For a moment they just stared at each other. Then she bent her head. "Well, I should return to the party."

"As you wish," he said. "I'll stay out on the terrace for a moment's air. I'm pleased we could resolve our differences and can now become neutral acquaintances rather than enemies. Good evening, Miss Lockhart."

"Good evening, my lord," she said, and wondered why her voice was suddenly rough. It must have been the autumn air, filled with dust from the falling leaves and smoke. She inclined her head and returned to the ball, feeling his gaze on her with every step.

And even though this conversation should have, in theory, made her feel better about everything, instead she felt something else. A vague discomfort, an odd misalignment, as if she no longer fit into her clothing or her skin anymore.

So even though she resolved not to be angry with him anymore, Clarissa still found herself looking forward to the moment when the Earl of Kirkwood would depart her presence and allow her to return to the person she was before she'd met him on her drive.

Roderick wasn't certain how long he stayed out on the terrace. At least a few songs from the orchestra played as he looked out over the moonlight garden below. He'd offered to remain here to give Clarissa...Miss Lockhart, an opportunity to return without his interference or company. But the longer he remained outside, the more his mind turned.

He had created a life where he didn't often brood. At least not about women he didn't even know. And yet the conversation with her replayed in his head over and over again. Her expressions of emotion, ones she kept repressing, danced before him. She was a fascinating creature, somehow. One he didn't *want* to be fascinated by.

He turned to go back to the ballroom and the terrace doors opened again. George stepped out, glanced over the terrace, and his expression lit up when he saw Roderick.

"There you are," he said. "I thought you'd run off with some woman or something."

Roderick almost snorted in response. He had done just that, he supposed, at least briefly. Though not the way his friend thought. "No, just getting some air," he said, and stepped toward George. "I was just coming back in."

"How are you enjoying yourself?" George asked as they reentered the hall with its crush of guests.

Miss Lockhart had asked the same thing a short time ago. For his friend, he gave a different answer. "It is much as you thought it would be. Not the worst country gathering I've been to, of course." He cleared his throat. "I did manage to get a moment with your cousin."

"With Clarissa?" George said in surprise. "I'm shocked you survived it. She glares daggers into you at every turn. Did you seduce a friend of hers or something?"

"That was my question, but it turns out it was exactly as I feared and warned you about upon our arrival. She was angry that I came uninvited. I thought, yet again, that you were going to clear the air about that with the family, but it's obvious you didn't."

George pulled a face of playful guilt. "Ugh, yes, I suppose I was. I hope you blamed me entirely."

"I did." Roderick folded his arms. "I swear, you are terrible. You let the woman hate me for days."

His friend's brow wrinkled. "I suppose. But...why do you care?"

"What?"

"Why do you care? You don't know my cousin, you'll likely rarely encounter her. She's too polite to spread nasty stories about you, for fear it would reflect poorly on her and her drive to be unfailingly well-mannered. She isn't your type, and even if she were, she's looking for marriage, not the sort of wickedly temporary arrangements you tend to make with ladies. Why would you care what she thinks of you?"

Roderick blinked. He'd spent so much time since his arrival being irritated with the woman, wanting to clear the air between them, he hadn't actually ever asked himself that very good question. Why *did* he care what she thought of him?

"I don't," he said. "I just don't like that I was blamed for something you did." He arched a playful brow. "This is exactly like school, you know."

George laughed. "Very well, I am in the wrong, I know. *Again.* Great God, though, the idea that she tempted you…"

"Of course not," Roderick said.

His mind went back to the terrace, when Miss Lockhart had looked up at him in the moonlight, her expression soft and fascinating eyes holding his. Perhaps there had been a bit of temptation, albeit brief, in that moment. But that was different. The woman was attractive, he was allowed to notice that. It didn't mean anything, though.

None of it meant anything at all.

CHAPTER 5

The following day, Clarissa sat one the same veranda where she had encountered Kirkwood the night before, but this time she had a cup of tea in her hand and was joined by the Marquess of Mickenshire, one of the potential suitors her parents had dragged out to the country for her to impress. She was trying not to yawn. Ladies did not yawn in public. Certainly they never gave any hint that they were bored. She wasn't even certain she was allowed to be bored. She would have to check her book later.

"At any rate, I've decided to have my tenants plant barley this year," the marquess was droning on.

She nodded and supposed that it was good the gentleman was so involved in matters of his estate. She didn't want to marry a layabout who had no interest in maintaining his responsibilities. But when she looked at the gentleman, her heart sank. He was older than her father.

"Lord Mickenshire," her mother called out, drawing the attention of the entire party toward her. "You must tell Clarissa about your *darling* grandchildren."

The marquess started at that demand and Clarissa's cheeks heated. Trust her mother to insert herself and make the age difference she had just been pondering all the more obvious.

"You've grandchildren?" she asked, though she knew the answer already.

"I have three," the marquess said. "My daughters are both married now. You may recall them."

She shifted. "I-I do. Though they came out a few years before I did."

Almost ten years. That was how wide the gap was between this man's youth and her own. Even his children were far older.

"Ah, yes, of course." The marquess appeared to be as uncomfortable as she was. After all, talk of his daughters had to make the entire party think of the fact that the marquess had no sons. He'd had two previous wives who had died trying to produce one so his title would live on without going to another part of his line.

Hence why he needed a young woman as bride so he could continue to try the same. She shivered at the thought. She knew little about the entire act that produced children, but enough to feel she didn't want to try it with this man.

"Will you excuse me, Miss Lockhart?" the marquess said with a tight smile as he rose.

She nodded and when he was gone, she caught her father's eye. He glared at her, as if she had frightened the man off, rather than her mother's heavy-handed intrusion into their conversation. She sighed. She was about to get up herself and freshen her tea when her cousin George flopped himself into the chair the marquess had departed.

"Dearest cousin," he said with a little chuckle. "It seems my aunt and uncle are much the same. Do they ever change?"

She stifled a smile. Once upon a time she and George had put their heads together and giggled over the sometimes awkward behavior of her parents. As the years ticked by, though, she found less humor in how their grasping seemed to frighten suitors off or how they increased the pressure on her to save them through marriage.

Besides, she wasn't supposed to feel or express such things about her parents. One was meant to receive what they presented with grace and gratitude.

"They mean well," she said softly even though the words tasted bitter on her tongue. "I must respect their methods, either way. They're my elders and deserve respect."

George's normally playful expression fell a fraction. "Clarissa."

She met his gaze and shrugged. "I must behave well."

"You've never done anything less," he said and covered her hand briefly. They were quiet together a moment as she enjoyed his company. For all his faults and frivolities, George had never made her feel pressured or judged. He shifted in his seat. "You offer them forgiveness. Will you do the same for me?"

She tilted her head in surprise at the question. "What have you done that needs—" She cut herself off and pursed her lips as she thought of her encounter with Kirkwood the night before. "Oh, you are talking about the earl."

He nodded. "I am. I've heard you've been judging him for my bad behavior."

She sucked in a breath. "He told you that, did he?"

She wanted to be annoyed that he'd done so. It almost felt like he'd tattled on her by running off to her cousin to declare their conversation. But then again, there was a tiny thrill that filled her at the idea that he'd spoken to George about her. It was ludicrous, but there even if she didn't wish it to be.

"He did," George admitted. "But even if he hadn't, it's been obvious. You're normally so welcoming to all comers, but you've been icy cold to him since our arrival."

She tensed at the idea that she'd been so noticeably rude. "Well, he's a rake, you know."

George leaned in closer. "So am I. And you like me."

She laughed. "I tolerate you, George. Barely."

He snorted out his own laugh, loud enough that others looked at them. "I deserve that. It was my fault, though, Clarissa. And I actually think you wouldn't hate my friend if you gave him a chance and got to know him."

She'd decided last night to try not to hate Kirkwood, but the idea she would get to know him settled oddly in her chest. "You want me to know him?"

He nodded. "I do."

"Why does it matter to you?"

For a moment George looked off into the crowd and she followed his gaze. He was looking at Kirkwood, who was standing across the way talking to Mrs. Vale. For a moment Clarissa narrowed her gaze at the sight, but then forced herself to stop.

"He's one of my best friends," George said. "And you are my favorite cousin. I wouldn't hate it if you two had a truce so that I could talk to both of you without having to run interference to keep you from coming to blows."

She laughed again at the idea of fisticuffs with the earl. She might have judged him as rude, but she couldn't picture him doing so. And he was enormous at any rate, far bigger than she was. She'd have to rise up on her tippy toes just to land a blow. Well, perhaps that was going too far.

She let her laughter trail off as Kirkwood looked at her. He stiffened a fraction, but then he smiled and inclined his head. "Very well. I agree to the truce. And if the opportunity arises I will, *reluctantly*, get to know the man. I assume we'll have nothing in common." She thought of what he'd said about *Othello* earlier and shook her head. "Or at least very little. But I'll try for you."

"Thank you, Clarissa," George said, and patted her hand. "Now I see your father weaving his way over, likely ready to give you a thousand suggestions on how to land yourself an *ancient* marquess and give him a son."

"Ugh," Clarissa said with a giggle she couldn't repress, etiquette rules or no. "That is crude."

"Do you want me to save you by sweeping you over there or not?" He pointed toward the far end of the veranda.

"Yes, please!" she admitted, and rose with him, took his arm and let him take her away just as he'd suggested. But she couldn't help but look over her shoulder, not toward her father, but in the direction of

Kirkwood. He'd stepped away from Mrs. Vale now and leaned against the terrace wall, one ankle crossed over another as he surveyed the rest of the party with casual elegance and perfected disinterest.

They would only be forced into a shared space for a limited time. If her cousin wanted her to try to like the man, she could do that. It didn't mean anything anyway.

Roderick didn't know what to think of the fact that Miss Lockhart was *smiling* at him as he and the other gentlemen entered the parlor after supper. She'd actually been doing that all day, ever since the earlier tea on the veranda.

He had decided she was either trying to make up for her initial misunderstanding, or she was plotting to poison him. He wasn't sure which one he believed more. He could see her doing either. Or both? She seemed interesting enough for that.

He pursed his lips at the errant thought just as she started across the parlor toward him.

"My lord," she said as she reached him.

"Miss Lockhart," he said with caution.

"How did you find my father's port?" she asked. "That is what you gentleman do when you part from the ladies, isn't it? Drink port and bluster?"

He hesitated before he said, "The port was very fine, yes. But there was little bluster this evening, instead we played billiards. I lost, but I enjoyed myself. I assume the ladies did…whatever it is ladies do when they find themselves relieved by the absence of men."

She smiled a little at his choice of phrase and he thought it might actually be a real expression. "It truly varies with the company and we swear an oath never to tell, you know. However, I can reveal to you that this group mostly gossiped about next Season's fashion in hats." She seemed to stifle a sigh.

"And did you come to a consensus about what will change?"

"More feathers," she whispered. "Do not tell a soul."

He laughed. "I'll be silent as the grave, I promise you."

Their shared laughter trailed off and her cheeks pinkened as she looked away from him and into the crowd. "I'm sure there will be parlor games in a moment. Do you have any favorites?"

He was utterly confused. She was interviewing him as if she intended to hire him for some duty. "It's the wrong time of year, but snapdragon is always a laugh."

She let out the faintest snort and shook her head. "That makes perfect sense."

"And what does *that* mean?"

She glanced at him. "You light a bowl of liquor on *fire*, then try to snatch raisins out of it without singeing your fingertips or eyebrows off. It's a reckless game."

"Ah, I see. So you judge me reckless. Willing to throw caution to the wind for...raisins." He smiled at her.

She huffed out a breath. "*You* brought it up."

"I did, I did." He arched a brow. If she was playing a game with him, he could do the same. "I've always liked Kiss the Monkey."

Her cheeks flamed higher and for good reason. It was a very wicked game, though played often in good company, where the lady and gentlemen would kneel with their backs to each other and arms linked, then attempt to kiss from that angle. He was very good at doing so, knew how to bend his body to catch a lady's lips with his.

"I-I've never played that one," she said, a little softer.

He wrinkled his brow. "No? Should I suggest it?"

"Oh...my lord, I'm not sure if—"

"What say we play a game!" Roderick called out with a mischievous wink for her. "Miss Lockhart and I have been discussing Kiss the Monkey."

There was a ripple through the crowd and varying expressions of excitement and disapproval. But Clarissa's father rushed forward, his eyes glittering as if this were his own plan. "Oh yes, my lord. A capital idea. What fun. And since you have suggested it, I believe you and my daughter must be the first to play."

Clarissa was pale now. "Father—"

"Come clear those chairs away," Mrs. Lockhart interrupted, waving at the servants. "It will open up a space."

Clarissa glanced at Roderick and all the teasing he'd been doing faded away. Her bottom lip was trembling, as if she were terrified. He'd never intended that, only to tweak her a little because getting her ire up was a little crack in that oh-so-proper façade.

"As they do that, let me strategize with the lady," he said, and drew her away from the giggling crowd of partygoers. She wouldn't look up at him now. "You appear sick," he said gently.

She shook her head. "I'm not. It's a party game. I suppose there is nothing terribly untoward about it. I only…" She trailed off.

"Only what?" he encouraged.

She lifted her gaze to him and for a moment he couldn't breathe. There was so much in those eyes, those lovely, unique brown-green eyes. All the emotions she was adept at suppressing shone at once. Pain and anger, worry and fear.

"What is it, Clarissa," he whispered, and then corrected himself. "Miss Lockhart?"

She swallowed. "I've…I've never been kissed."

He blinked. George had said this was her third Season out when they spoke about her in London. That would make her in her very early twenties. He hadn't imagined that some green boy hadn't stolen a sweet kiss in all those years. She was a tempting beauty, after all.

"I see," he said, and pondered his options. "In that case, I'll lose the game."

She blinked. "What?"

"I only suggested it to tease you, but I can see now that it wasn't fair given the circumstances. So I'll lose the game and miss in my attempt to kiss you."

Her brow wrinkled. "I—"

She did not have time to finish her response. Her mother rushed over, grabbed her arm and began to drag her into the circle the guests had made for the game. "Come, you two. It's time to begin!"

He knelt down on the floor and turned his back as she began to do the same. He felt her tremble as she linked one arm through his and then the other. The press of her back to his own was warm, and he could feel her sharp intakes of breath as they tried to position themselves best. It was a challenge, for she was petite and they didn't exactly align perfectly, even on their knees. But then, that was part of the challenge of the game.

"Ready?" Mr. Lockhart asked, and then cried out, "Kiss the Monkey!"

They each twisted, rolling their upper bodies around for a moment, trying to find the proper way to partially face each other without breaking the link of their arms. At last Roderick found himself with an angle that would allow him to reach her lips. She had wetted them as they struggled and for the first time he noticed how full the lower one was. Her eyes shone as she stared at him, trying to fake a smile like this was fun when he could see that she was nervous. He leaned in, attempting not to make the moment where he missed her lips too obvious.

But to his surprise she tilted her head, and instead of dodging him, their mouths met.

It was the briefest and most chaste of kisses. Their lips grazed, perfectly fitted even in the awkward position. Hers were warm, soft, and he had the oddest urge to fully face her and let the kiss linger a bit longer. But he couldn't. The party laughed and clapped as she turned her face away and they unlinked arms. Her cheeks were flamed dark red, but she allowed him to help her to her feet as he, too, rose. She stared at him a moment, then stepped away.

"Who—who is next?" she asked with false lightness for the group. "George, you look too wicked not to play. And Mrs. Vale, why don't you partner with him?"

She wasn't looking at Roderick as she gamely arranged the next round, but he couldn't stop looking at her. She had told him she'd never been kissed, so that meant he was the first man to have done so. She couldn't have wanted that, not when their relationship was, so far, adversarial. And yet *she* had been the one to meet his lips.

They were dizzying facts. Only because he didn't understand them, though. The kiss didn't warrant any further consideration. So he instead focused on his friend as George and Mrs. Vale laughingly took their place in the circle, nearly falling over as they tried to meet in the middle just as Roderick and Clarissa had.

But he didn't feel fully connected to the others as many took turns, to varying degrees of success and failure. No, he felt like he'd been dunked in water or was standing outside of glass looking in. And the woman who had put him there still refused to meet his gaze as she stood by the fireplace, picking at a loose thread on her gown sleeve.

It was all very odd, indeed.

CHAPTER 6

Clarissa rose early the next morning. Well, that wasn't entirely true. She'd found sleep almost impossible to find all night and had finally surrendered herself at just after dawn. Now readied, she sat in the library, a place where she had always been able to find stability and calm, and stared at the book in her hand with unseeing eyes.

She couldn't concentrate. No, all she could do was replay the moment in the parlor the night before when she had stared into the Earl of Kirkwood's eyes and wanted, with brief but overwhelming power, for him to kiss her. Propriety and etiquette and rules about a lady's comportment had all gone out the window and she had thwarted his attempt to save her from the embarrassment of the kiss.

How could one be so moved by such a brief thing? Such a *small* thing? Just the barest brush of flesh. She'd had more intimate contact with a dance partner as they pivoted on the floor at an assembly. And yet that kiss was something that haunted her.

Even now she could still feel the brief, gentle press of him on her lips, which she touched with her fingertips. Shouldn't they have changed color or felt hot? Anything to signify that she was different now, even if she didn't wish to be?

"There you are!"

She glanced up with a start and found her mother at the library door. Violet Lockhart was still a lovely woman, with a curvaceous figure and thick dark hair the same color as Clarissa's own. She always moved like a nervous butterfly, though. Always flitting, always darting, a ball of chaotic energy that could land upon anything, disrupt it and move on before anything could be righted.

Clarissa saw a certain expression on her mother's face and nervousness immediately spread in her chest. "It is early, Mama," she said, rising to properly greet her with a little bow of her head. "You are not normally out of bed at this hour."

"How could one sleep when there is so much excitement to be celebrated?" Mrs. Lockhart asked and slipped the book from Clarissa's fingers to toss it aside. Clarissa winced. It was a common theme in this house. What she wanted was not valued. But resenting that was against Societal expectation, so she had to shove it all down.

"The gathering is going well," she said carefully. "I think you deserve to celebrate your triumph."

"It could be better," Mrs. Lockhart said with a wave of her hand. "I think you should do your hair differently, my dear. It's so dull the way you've worn it the last few nights. And you had such a sour expression after the kissing game. You know men are only attracted to honey, so you mustn't *ever* put out vinegar."

"Yes, Mama," Clarissa said, and stifled a sigh. There seemed never to be an end to the unrequested advice and criticisms. Even when she succeeded, she failed.

"And yet, despite any little mistakes you've made, all is not lost." Her mother grasped her hand. "I could have slapped your cousin in the face for bringing an uninvited guest to our soiree. I had to change all the chamber assignments at the last moment. But now I could kiss George instead, for the Earl of Kirkwood offers us a grand opportunity."

Nausea rolled through Clarissa in a wave and she swallowed hard.

"You and Father keep saying that despite how poorly matched we are. What—what do you mean?"

But she knew what her mother meant, even before Mrs. Lockhart said it. All her machinations were plain on her face. "Poorly matched? He is the finest catch here, Clarissa. You must see that. And I've watched you two together. The pall-mall game? When you danced at the ball? And then the kissing game last night? There is a marriage ripe for the making."

Clarissa stood on shaky knees and stared at her mother. "Mama, you cannot be serious."

Mrs. Lockhart appeared confused. "I'm perfectly serious, of course."

Clarissa paced away, clenching and unclenching her hands as she tried to remain calm. Serene. Proper. All she wanted to do was scream. "If you have been watching as closely as you claim, you must also see that Kirkwood and I *do not* suit."

"What do you mean?"

"We are entirely different. We don't *like* each other, even if we have managed to move into the realm of toleration."

Her mother stared up at her without leaving her seat and she seemed entirely bewildered when she said, "What does that matter?"

Tears stung Clarissa's eyes. That question about her needs, her emotions, her desires, had always hung in the air between her and her parents. But it had never been stated so plainly. Normally they at least pretended that what they desired was for her own good, her best interest, trying to convince her that she had truly wanted it all along.

But in her thrill at the idea of the match, Mrs. Lockhart made it clear that no one was actually considering Clarissa any more than they would a chess piece on a board. Easily sacrificed.

"He is a well-known rake," Clarissa said, and wished she couldn't hear the edge of pain in her voice. "Even the debutantes hear whispers of his long list of former lovers. That he once brought one of the most scarlet courtesans to a royal event. That he wagers at cards in shocking places. And yet you have insisted that *I* must behave properly. You have plied me with book after book on the subject of comportment. How could you now wish to link me to such a man?"

"He has over ten thousand a year from his estates alone, a well-established title and links to every important family in the country," her mother said as she got up at last. "Gracious, you are being silly and very selfish. Think of your parents and all the ways you could help us when you are countess. And a man is allowed to be a rake, my dear. Your behavior doesn't have anything to do with his." She smoothed her skirt and started for the door. "You are not getting younger, Clarissa. A match is imperative before all the bloom goes off the rose. Your father and I expect you to behave as if you understand that. Now I'm off to make sure the breakfast room is ready for our guests."

She swept out of the room in a cloud of schemes. The nausea Clarissa had felt upon her mother's entry into the library multiplied now, making her dizzy and hot with the sinking sickness that she had no control over her own life. That her parents would arrange it so she never could.

She rushed from the room and turned toward the backstairs so she could flee to her chamber to calm herself, but because she wasn't looking she crashed headlong into a person she hadn't seen coming the other way up the hallway.

Large, strong hands caught her, dragging her a little closer and she looked up to find herself practically in the arms of the very man her mother had just been scheming to land as Clarissa's husband: the Earl of Kirkwood.

After a night of surprisingly tormenting dreams about the very woman who Roderick now steadied in his arms, he felt discombobulated by the fact that she had careened into him at far too early an hour for most ladies of her rank. He was going to defuse the moment with a joke, but then she gazed up at him and her expression stopped him in his tracks.

She looked like an animal who had just realized they'd been caged. Her eyes were dark and shiny with unshed tears, her pupils dilated, her hands shaking and her cheeks pale.

"Clarissa," he whispered, reverting to her given name without thought.

She yanked away from him. "Don't!" she burst out, and staggered back into the room she had fled from less than a moment before.

He followed her and found it was the library. "What is it?"

"None of your business," she snapped without looking at him.

He tensed. It seemed they were enemies again. He wondered why that stung so much. It wasn't as if he hadn't predicted that after last night and her avoidance of him after their kiss. Hardly a kiss at that. Nothing more than a brush of lips. And yet her obvious pain made him feel increasingly guilty about it.

"I'm sorry about my behavior in the parlor," he began.

"What?" She pivoted toward him and stared.

"Kiss the Monkey. I don't know you well enough to tease you so. I was as rude as you've accused me to be since my arrival and—"

She waved her hand. "That doesn't matter."

"You aren't upset about the kiss?" he asked.

"No. *I foolishly kissed you.*"

She flushed a little, then bent her head and her breathing came shallow. He stepped closer. "If that isn't what's troubling you, then what is? Your upset is plain and I wish to help if I can."

"You cannot help me," she gasped as she pushed past him toward the door. "In fact, I would advise you to stay far away from me, my lord. And I'll do the same with you."

Then she was gone. He moved to the door, but she was already halfway up the hallway, not looking back, not slowing as she made her escape. He stepped back into the library and shook his head. He had no idea what had caused her to react this way. He ought not to have cared. He'd offered assistance, as was gentlemanly, and she had refused. Now he should take her advice, back his way out of all this and simply let the time that remained in the gathering tick by. Afterward he'd just forget her, go back to his life and, he hoped, eventually meet the woman who would be the lightning bolt to his heart.

And yet he stared at the door to the chamber where she had left, his mind uneasy and stomach turning. For some unfathomable reason, he liked Miss Clarissa Lockhart. And the idea that she was so miserable didn't sit right with him. Whether it was his place to feel that way or not.

~

"I must make a plan," Clarissa said as she paced her chamber later in the day.

She was already dressed for supper and the entertainments afterward. Her mother had insisted she would play her harp for the gathering first. Oh, how she hated the harp. She'd been forced to play it for years, having instructors stand over her, rapping her knuckles if she plucked a string wrong. There was no pleasure in it for her.

But there was also no denying her parents. So she would do it, exhibit like a circus animal who did tricks. All to catch a man.

All to catch *Kirkwood*, if her parents had their way. She increased her pacing as the panic she had been fighting all day rose again in her chest. Matched with Kirkwood, a man who was her polar opposite, a rake and a rogue who cared little for propriety. What kind of marriage would that make? They could only discuss *Othello* for so long and then?

"I *must* make a plan," she said again. "I must make a plan to entice one of the other gentlemen at the gathering. One who would make a better match. If I do so, Mama and Father will have no choice but to allow for it. They'll harangue me about the missed opportunity, but they'll settle for what they have and that will be the end of it."

Yes, that was it. She had to do that.

Only she wasn't certain how. How did a lady maintain decorum while also pursuing a mate? How did one force a gentleman into seeing *her* as a future wife without being too flashy or loud or forward? Without discussing inappropriate topics or laughing too loudly or showing too much skin and all while wearing white, white, white to show off her modesty?

There was a light knock on her door and she pivoted toward it. Who could it be? Hester, her maid, had come and gone long ago to prepare her and her mother had seemed distracted since making her statement that a match with Kirkwood would be best. Would she come back now and further her cause?

"Who—who is it?" Clarissa choked out.

"It's Marianne. Er, Lady Ramsbury."

Clarissa caught her breath and rushed to the door, trying to put serenity back on her face for the sake of the countess. She threw open the door and knew she'd failed when Marianne's expression fell.

"Oh, gracious," she said as she stepped into Clarissa's room and shut the door. "What's wrong?"

"Nothing." Clarissa fought for further calm. "I'm fine as can be, I assure you. I'm only making my final preparations for supper and the musical presentations tonight. Are you going to play, my lady?"

Marianne tilted her head. "Clarissa."

"Yes?"

"You have nearly worried your handkerchief in half," she said gently.

Clarissa looked down. She'd forgotten she was holding a handkerchief, but Marianne was right. She had shredded the fabric almost in two. "Oh."

"Something is wrong," Marianne said. "I felt it all day. You were so quiet and seemed nervous."

"Oh no," Clarissa murmured. "That's not right. A lady is to have moderation in all things. One mustn't be able to sense her emotions too strongly."

Marianne shook her head. "I...I don't know what to say to that. Emotions are a human fact. They aren't wrong."

"No, Lady Ramsbury—"

"Marianne," she interrupted. "You and I knew each other a little over the years. You must call me Marianne, for I want us to be friends."

"You see, that right there," Clarissa said, and paced away. "It isn't right for me to be so forward as to call you by your given name when your rank demands I address you properly. How am I to be polite by acquiescing to what you've asked *and* be proper and correct by the rules of Society all at once? How can one be meekly sportive? How? They are opposites!"

Marianne caught her hands. "You are upsetting yourself further. Please sit down with me and take a few breaths."

Clarissa stared at her a moment and then nodded. "Yes. I'm—I'm sorry, my lady. Marianne. You've caught me at an…an odd moment."

They sat on the settee by her fire and for a moment Marianne just breathed with her. Then she said, "Why don't you tell me what's troubling you? Perhaps I could help. Or at least listen."

Clarissa worried her lip. She did so want to tell someone what was happening. To get advice from someone who wasn't an interested party like her parents, or an *uninterested* one like her cousin. George would make a joke out of all of it, which would lighten her mood, but not in any way help her solve her problem.

"Are you certain you would want to hear my troubles?" she asked. "I don't feel right burdening you."

"It's no burden," Marianne insisted, and squeezed her hand. "I understand how difficult it can be when one is trying to hold everything inside and there aren't friends around for the release of confession. Please allow me to be of service, and tell me. I promise I won't repeat anything you reveal."

"Even to the earl?" she asked, thinking of how Ramsbury and Kirkwood were friends.

"I do tell Sebastian everything, he is my dearest friend," Marianne said slowly. "But in this case, since it isn't my secret, I don't see why I would have any reason to share."

Clarissa considered that a moment. Despite the promise, she would simply be careful not to reveal too many details so that Marianne wouldn't be able to determine that her problem was Kirkwood. What would he think of her if he knew her mother's machinations?

"I think everything is aware that I am seeking a husband."

Marianne nodded. "As we are expected to do by Society."

Clarissa flinched. Society's expectations were feeling especially weighty at present and she had to fight not to return to the state where she could hardly breathe from the pressure.

"My parents arranged this gathering as a way for me to further that goal. Not unusual, but their demands have increased in the last few months." She shook her head. "I thought I had time before they simply took matters into their own hands, but today…today…"

She couldn't continue, she was so choked on tears that she couldn't allow to fall. Marianne squeezed her hand again. "Go on."

"My—my mother has declared that there is a specific match she wants me to pursue here at the gathering," she said slowly.

"Oh. I see," Marianne said with a frown. "And it isn't a gentleman *you* are interested in?"

A vision of Lord Kirkwood seemed to shimmer in Clarissa's mind. So tall and handsome, so utterly infuriating and also charming. And surprising in a great many ways, for he could be chivalrous and apologetic when one least expected it.

"I don't think we'd be a good fit," she said. "For a great many reasons."

Marianne nodded, her expression troubled. "Arranged marriages are still the common way for those in our rank. But just because it's considered normal doesn't mean it's right. I hate it, for I think it shuts the door for ladies and gentlemen to find love."

"Oh no," Clarissa said with a swift shake of her head. "I *never* expected to find love. I don't need it." She said it and it felt cold on her tongue, but she continued, "I always assumed I would match with someone I could bear, someone who would have some things in common with me so that we wouldn't bore each other in the first month of marriage, someone who would offer as much as he received from the bargain."

Marianne almost looked sad at that assessment, but she nodded as if to encourage Clarissa to carry on, so she did. "I thought I would be allowed the opportunity to choose that gentleman myself. Of course, I may only pick from the men they throw in my path, but still. It wouldn't be a march down an aisle toward a man who is so entirely infuriating and opposite to me."

Marianne tilted her head. "Who is the encouraged match?"

Clarissa bit her lip. The countess was being so entirely kind that she wanted to say, but she thought again of the link between Ramsbury and Kirkwood and instead shook her head. "It is better not to reveal him."

Marianne hesitated and then nodded. "I understand. Is there something I can do to help?"

Clarissa sighed. "When you found me here, I was pacing my room trying to come up with a plan. *Any* plan to avoid the machinations of my parents."

"I suppose the best plan would be to find a match with someone else. Someone you feel is better suited to *your* goals."

"Yes," Clarissa said in relief. "That was exactly what I determined, myself. My only trouble is I don't know who to choose and I also have no idea how to encourage a man to match. I've had no luck so far, after all."

Marianne nodded. "Well, let us think about the potentials here at the party. There is Lord Crossworth. He is of an age with you and isn't difficult to look at."

"But I bested him at pall-mall," Clarissa said with a shake of her head. "He was very angry that afternoon and has avoided me ever since. I think I ruined my chance there."

The countess made a little sound in her throat. "If he couldn't take good competition, then he doesn't deserve you anyway."

"Does that mean you best Lord Ramsbury at games?" Marianne said with a blink.

Marianne's smile widened. "I think Sebastian would be more offended if I let him win than if I bested him. A good partner will enjoy seeing you at your best. He certainly shouldn't be troubled by a challenge."

Once again, Clarissa thought of Kirkwood and how they had battled to let each other win on the pall-mall field. He had made it fun to compete, and yes, he had been bothered that she allowed him to win.

But no, he was exactly who she *shouldn't* match with.

"I think Lord Crossworth must be dismissed," Clarissa sighed.

"What about Mr. Longford? He's the second son of the Earl of Mulgrave."

Clarissa worried her lip. "He hasn't paid me much attention since his arrival. We've only danced once. I suppose I could try a little harder. But I do worry, Marianne, because of his rank. The gentleman my mother insists is the one for me has a title. If I come to her with this man, she'll feel I took a step down."

"I see." Marianne let out her breath in a long exhale. "Well, if that's the trouble, then we will eliminate many of the gentlemen here. Lord Anthony and Mr. Townshend are also second sons, so the trouble would be the same."

"That leaves us with the Marquess of Mickenshire."

Marianne met her eyes. "You realize that by naming all your potentials, or not naming one, I can deduce who it is you are trying to avoid."

Clarissa gasped. She'd been so upset she hadn't thought that part through. "Oh, you must think me foolish."

"What is wrong with Kirkwood?" Marianne asked gently. "He is far closer to your age, is intelligent, handsome and he is an old friend of my husband's, so I can vouch for his character, no matter the rake he chooses to play."

"I don't think he's looking for a bride, first off," Clarissa said. "But even if he were, he wouldn't want it to be me any more than I would wish it to be him, I think. We started off on the wrong foot upon his arrival. I may have realized he isn't the person I believed him to be then, but we are so opposite each other in temperament and how we believe we should move through the world. How could that ever be a good union?"

"I have very different views about marriage than you do, I think," Marianne said after a pause. "My brother never dreamed of forcing a union on me that I would not want. When I had no success on my own, I gave up on the idea that there would be a man for me. But Sebastian and I fell in love under very odd circumstances. I can tell you that a friend becoming a lover is a wonderful thing. And that a rake with a wallflower, or at least someone far more proper than himself, can also be a wonderful match. You seem a very intelligent person. I think you underestimate the charm of someone who challenges you. Who isn't exactly like you in the way they view the world."

Clarissa swallowed. She'd always seen a marriage as a transaction. She'd been taught that since her youth, had never dared to dream of something more. She wasn't about to start now, even if there was something bewitching to the tale Marianne spun.

"It wouldn't work for me," Clarissa said softly. "And so that leaves me with Mickenshire."

Marianne's lips pursed. "I can say nothing untoward about the man, but that he is so much older than you are, my dear. And his desires for his marriage are patently clear."

"He wants his heir, yes." Clarissa blushed. She knew very little about how that was acquired, but what she did know didn't make her feel better about this. "I would do my best to provide that. His rank would appease my parents and he certainly is viewed with great respect."

"Because he's older than Zeus, himself," Marianne said with a dry chuckle. "One must respect someone who has been around since the beginning of time immemorial."

Clarissa giggled despite herself. "He isn't *that* ancient. You are very wicked."

"But it made you laugh, so it was worth it." Marianne grasped her hand again. "I can see you're a woman who cannot be deterred when you make your mind up. And I understand what it's like to be in an untenable position. So if I can help you land your gentleman, I will if you'd like."

Clarissa shifted in her place. "I'd be grateful for your assistance."

And she was. But there was something in her chest that made that statement feel like a lie. A sinking horror at the idea that she might actually succeed at making a match with the marquess. Not because she thought him terrible, of course, but because she realized how little she was interested in the man.

But her interest didn't matter, did it? Attraction was a lark that would fade anyway. What she needed was a longer-term stability and a matching of temperaments. It was time to stop mincing around and do her duty, before it was done for her.

"Thank you," she said. "You are too good."

Marianne nodded as they rose together, but she didn't look certain. And any certainty Clarissa felt was fleeting and forced. But this was her life. She was going to lead it.

CHAPTER 7

It had been two days since Roderick encountered Clarissa outside the library and she warned him away. And she had been true to her word and avoided him strenuously ever since. Or at least as well as she could. They'd been seated next to each other at supper once in that time, though she had only briefly spoken to him and hadn't met his eyes.

She'd been much more verbose and friendly with another of the partygoers. The very man she was standing with now, across the garden, chatting away with a serene smile on her face like he was the most interesting person in the world: the Marquess of Mickenshire.

Roderick pursed his lips. He had no idea why Clarissa was putting so much of her attention on the man. Mickenshire was boring as plain toast, certainly not matched to her wit and the fire she tried so hard to hide from everyone around her.

George stepped up beside him and offered him punch. He took it but didn't drink. "Did something happen regarding your cousin?"

George blinked and looked toward her in the crowd. "Not that I know of. Why do you ask?"

"I've simply noticed her putting a great deal of attention into the marquess." Roderick motioned toward them. "And I sometimes sense a little desperation in the way she interacts with him. She laughs too hard at what cannot be interesting stories. She ignores it when he treads on her feet while they dance."

George's lips pursed and he observed the marquess and Clarissa a moment. "Hmm. She does seem to be paying particular attention to the man, you are right. I don't know why—she doesn't talk to me about such things, of course. But I do know my aunt and uncle are singular. They've been pressing harder and harder on her to marry and marry well in the last year. Perhaps she has decided to acquiesce at last and has chosen the marquess as her way out of their noose."

Roderick flinched at the idea. For Clarissa to *marry* Mickenshire? She couldn't possibly be happy with such a life.

"I suppose if she did choose him," George continued, "at least the union would likely be brief. If she can produce him his heir, she'll be well taken care of in the end."

That was true. At his age, Mickenshire would likely have ten years left if he was lucky. But he couldn't see Clarissa being so mercenary. Her attention to propriety wouldn't allow for it, if nothing else.

"I do not understand these parents who will sacrifice their children, especially their daughters, in such a way," he said with a scowl. "Brief or not, can they possibly be happy with the idea of her marrying a man older than her father who will only see her as a broodmare?"

Now it was George who flinched. "I agree, it's not palatable. But I've no say in the matter. The higher title and the money that comes with it is tied up with my parents until I inherit and you know my father is hale and hearty. I cannot do anything to support Clarissa away from the desires of her parents. Even if I could, she is so driven to be meek to their demands thanks to those awful comportment books...she might bend to their will even if she saw another exit to the situation." George shook his head. "This is entirely depressing. I think I'll get another drink."

George strode off and Roderick pursed his lips harder as he continued to stare at Clarissa. That serene smile that tilted her lips didn't reach her eyes. She almost looked...haunted, and his stomach turned on her behalf. She stepped away, out of his view and he realized her father was standing behind her. And Mr. Lockhart was watching...*him* evenly and with purpose. Roderick shifted and dropped his gaze away.

Did Mr. Lockhart resent his attention to Clarissa? Fear that he might intrude upon the match he and his wife so desired? And why did Roderick wish to intrude? He wasn't going to marry Clarissa, himself. He barely knew her, she didn't like him. And yet he wished very much to discuss this matter with her. To try to convince her that her future didn't have to be so *pallid*. Mickenshire was pallid, as plain as Clarissa's gowns.

He found her in the crowd again. She was crossing away from the group, across the lawn and around toward the back of the house. He drew a brief breath and followed, setting his drink down on the edge of a table as he exited the party.

When he came around the house, he didn't see her for a moment, but then he caught a glimpse of her gown as she disappeared into one of the doors that led back into the house. He walked faster to catch up with her and entered the house as she made her way down the hallway. She hadn't noticed him yet, it seemed, but he noticed everything about her. There was nothing calm in the way she walked, hands clenched at her sides, body stiff as she moved. She was upset, just as she had been when they last spoke in the library.

It seemed the library would be the same place they would speak today for she staggered into the room out of his sight. He drew a few long breaths as he slowed his pace. He had a choice here. He could do as she'd requested days ago and leave her alone. He could go back to the party, pretend he hadn't seen her unraveling. Or he could follow. Insert himself where he didn't belong. He could try to help her, though he'd never considered himself any great hero to ladies.

He couldn't stop himself, it seemed. He entered the library behind her.

~

Clarissa couldn't draw a full breath as she entered the library. Once this had been her sanctuary, but she had found no pleasure in it for days. She found no pleasure in anything, truth be told.

She had been raised to marry for position, but now that she was making headway with the marquess…and she *was* making headway with him, she could feel his interest increasing…she felt sick. There was no attraction whatsoever there for her. When she looked at him, she was put to mind of her dear grandfather, not of a husband. And he was boring, so boring. He repeated himself and talked over her and had no interest in anything modern or fun. All he *did* have interest in was producing an heir. He wasn't crude about it, of course he wouldn't be. But he did keep making not-so-subtle inquiries about her health. She kept expecting him to check her teeth like she was some pony he was considering buying.

She leaned against the bookshelf with one arm, rested her head in the crook and began to cry. She hadn't expected that to happen, but she did. And then she couldn't stop. Great heaving sobs wracked her entire body, a dam burst that she had likely been holding back for years. There was no moderation to be had in that moment, there was only pain and regret, fear and sadness.

She felt a hand on her arm, someone gently turning her and then strong arms encased her, tucking her against a firm, warm chest that smelled like sandalwood and mint and everything delicious. She glanced up to find it was Kirkwood. But of course it was Kirkwood. She'd known that, hadn't she? Even without seeing his face.

She should have pulled away, but instead she buried her head into his shoulder and allowed the tears to continue to flow. He stroked her hair gently, not saying a word to urge her to stop this foolish display. He merely witnessed it, allowing her to express it without judgment.

She had no idea how long they stood like that, but her sobs began to subside after some time. She realized she was clenching her fingers against his back and stopped.

He drew in a deep breath and she found herself doing the same, feeling some of the shattering emotion dissipate a little when she did.

"Tell me," he whispered at last.

She shook her head. She shouldn't tell him. Not him of all people. But the words were coming now, as uncontrollable as the tears and the feelings she always held back with all her might.

"I'll never have anything, will I?" she gasped out. "I realize what an empty, loveless life it will be. A passionless, so-very-proper, *empty* life."

Was that it? Was that what hurt so much? She'd always told herself, told Marianne, told anyone who asked, that she didn't require those connections in her husband. That she knew her duty and that arranged marriages were often transactional and cool.

And yet there was some wicked, improper part of herself that wanted more.

Kirkwood made a rumble from deep in his chest and then he cupped her chin, turning her face up toward him. "There is so much more in life than this, Clarissa," he said, his fingers splaying against her cheek gently. "You deserve so much more than this, don't you understand that? So much more than a man like the marquess could ever provide."

She blinked. His face was very close now. As close as it had been during the parlor games days before. When they'd kissed. Barely kissed. And like then, she realized she wished she could kiss him again. Not sweetly or briefly, but truly be kissed.

"Clarissa," he said, and his voice was rougher. He was lowering his head toward her, she was lifting her chin toward him, like they were called to each other by some unseen force. Their lips met.

At first it was very similar to the kiss in the game. Soft, gentle, just a brushing of lips. But then he made a possessive sound from his chest and his fingers moved up from her cheek and into her hair, tilting her face as his mouth pressed a little harder. She gasped at the sensation and her lips parted against his. His tongue darted out, tracing the opening she'd created, setting off fireworks of sensation through her entire being that were unlike anything she'd ever known.

She clung to him harder, leaning into his solidness, his strength, letting him guide her away from safety and into something like a warm bath that she could sink away into and never come out.

He tasted her, still gentle but now so intimate, and she found herself meeting him with her tongue, matching his strokes, lifting against him as the kiss deepened because she wanted more. More and more until there was nothing but this.

He pulled her closer, her body molding to his, his breath short and hot between kisses, his hands gripping at her like he was fighting for control. Was *she* stealing his control? His? That couldn't be right. And the triumph that wicked idea left in her couldn't be right either.

Somehow it didn't feel wrong, though. There was only sensation, not judgment. Beautiful, tingling, heated sensation that crept its way through her entire body and made her feel weightless.

She lifted against him again, seeking more of this, but before she could receive it, before she could come to her own senses and back away, before he could sweep her into whatever came next, there was a gasp at the library door.

They tore apart from each other and both stared toward the noise, only to find Clarissa's mother and father, along with their vicar, Mr. Reade, who had been in attendance at the garden party. All three were staring. Mr. Reade looked horrified and judgmental, but her parents, oh, that was a different story. Her mother was smiling, simply unable to cover her absolute delight in this humiliation and what it would cause. Her father at least had the decency to frown, even though his eyes danced.

Clarissa began to shake as she staggered backward, into the bookshelf, sending a few volumes clattering down onto the floor. She glanced at Kirkwood, who looked as shocked as she felt, and then her knees went out from under her and she slid toward the floor.

CHAPTER 8

Roderick caught Clarissa's arm as she began to collapse and supported her as best he could when his own world was spinning.

"There now," he murmured. "It's all right. Breathe."

She did so, but barely, and she shook her head at him, almost as if she could will what was happening away. But neither of them could. In what felt like half-time, Mr. and Mrs. Lockhart burst fully into the room together, arms flailing and voices barking at once.

"Sir, you have gone too far," Mr. Lockhart shouted, even as Mrs. Lockhart reached for Clarissa and dragged her away roughly. Clarissa tripped over the edge of the carpet with the sudden, violent movement, but her mother didn't stop.

"My poor child!" she said, but Roderick realized she was *smiling* as she spoke. Smiling. His heart sank, his stomach turned. Was this a trap? He had always avoided those so deftly. But not today.

He almost feared looking at Clarissa, feared seeing that she had been involved if this was what he believed. But when he did, he saw her cheeks were bloodless, her eyes glassy and shocked. That reaction seemed real, that horror and fear. Certainly her pain while she wept had felt real.

And her kiss? Oh, that had felt very real. And far more powerful than he could have imagined after she'd spent the entire party sniping at him.

He shook that thought away and forced himself to pay attention to what was happening around him.

"Please," he said, and his voice sounded thick. Mrs. Lockhart continued shrieking and he lifted a hand. "Madam, *please*. Lower your voice. We don't need the whole party to be aware of this, it will only cause more trouble and a scandal I would hope you wish to avoid for your daughter's sake, if nothing else."

Both the Lockharts appeared confused by that notion, for clearly neither were thinking of their daughter now. Had they ever? By this behavior, he had to guess no.

"Clarissa," he said gently. "Please sit before you fall over."

She swallowed hard, her gaze flitting to his, holding there. She was seeking, searching him. What did she find, he wondered. At last, though, she extracted herself from her mother's grip, one that had left red finger marks on her upper arm, and staggered to a chair before the fire where she took a place and then covered her face with her hands.

Her father, who hadn't even looked toward his daughter, folded his arms. "My lord, you have disgraced my daughter with the shocking display that we have all intruded upon."

Roderick ran a hand through his hair. "I agree, to kiss her was imprudent."

Clarissa didn't look up from her hands, but her shoulders shuddered a little. In agreement?

"Imprudent?" Mrs. Lockhart repeated, and then snorted. "Why, I believe if we had intruded even a few moments later, we would have found her with her innocence taken!"

"Mama!" Clarissa gasped, and now she did look up from her hands. Where before her expression had been pale, her cheeks were now dark red with humiliation.

The vicar stepped forward, holding up his hands as if to calm the situation. "Now, now. We needn't get into detail about all this. We all know what we saw. And perhaps if this had been a simple kiss on a terrace it might be something ignorable. And yet you two were in a chamber alone, and the kiss was quite…quite…"

"Filthy is what it was," Mr. Lockhart provided, and shook his head not at Roderick but at Clarissa. "I am entirely disappointed."

"Are you?" Clarissa said softly, and glanced up again, this time at her father. "Because your eyes say otherwise. How could you do this? How could you?"

Roderick bit back a gasp. It seemed she believed the same intentions from this intrusion as he did.

"There is only one solution now," her mother said, stepping forward with her hands fluttering. She was smiling again. Roderick didn't think she even knew she was doing it. "You must marry."

And there it was. Roderick's stomach turned and Clarissa let out a low, pained moan, like an animal who had been injured.

"Quite right," Mr. Lockhart blustered. "If you two were doing such a thing in the library with the door not even fully closed, what else might you have already done? Compromised, that's what you are, Clarissa. *Compromised*, and there is a toll to be paid for such a thing. I demand it, my lord."

Clarissa turned her gaze to Roderick and slightly shook her head. She might as well have screamed *no* at him. Grabbed his legs and begged him to set her free.

He feared he couldn't. No, the trap had been sprung on both of them.

"How could you do this?" Clarissa whispered. "How could you two do this to this man? To *me*?"

"You did it to yourself," Mr. Lockhart said with a sniff. "All that expense and work to make you a proper lady and instead you act like a common—"

Roderick stepped forward then and put himself in front of Clarissa, as if he could stop the sling of an arrow he feared would pierce her heart.

"Enough," he said. "Enough." He drew a shaky breath. "You will not blame her for something that is my fault. I found her in the library, I..." He thought briefly of the sight of her, leaning against the library shelves, sobbing. All he'd wanted to do was comfort her. "*I* lost control. And yes, given the reaction, I understand perfectly what needs to be done."

She rose behind him and clasped his arm with both her hands, tugging him so that he faced her. "Oh, no! Kirkwood, no!"

He stared down into her face. It was streaked with tears, pink with continued humiliation, her eyes were wide with fear and horror. She was lovely somehow, in the midst of it all. He had kissed her because she was lovely. And yet neither of them wanted this. All his dreams were about to die.

"We must marry, Clarissa," he said, as gently as he could manage when his heart felt like it was being torn in two. "I've created a situation where there is no choice but to marry."

Once when she was five, Clarissa had fallen from a boat into the lake. Under the water, she had heard her mother screaming, heard the men shouting, and then she had been hauled back to the surface. In that moment, it was the same. The sounds were hitting her ears. Words she couldn't fully understand because they felt like they were coming from outside the bubble where she was waiting to be saved.

Then her mother grabbed her arm and shook her back to reality. "Oh, congratulations, my love!"

Clarissa stared at her. Mrs. Lockhart looked so thrilled. Like this was the happiest of occasions, not something to be mourned. Worse, it made her family's machinations all the clearer and from Kirkwood's narrowed gaze, he knew that as well as she did.

How much he despised Clarissa for it remained to be seen.

He shook off her father's attempt at congratulations and said, "I would like to speak to my future bride. Alone."

Her father had the gall to laugh at that and slap Kirkwood on the shoulder. "No harm in it now, eh? But don't forget, you've made your statement that you will marry her in front of the vicar. That is the same as saying it to God, Himself."

"I've no intention on going back on my statement, *sir*," Kirkwood said, the frost on every word. "I don't go back on my promises."

He said that while he turned his gaze back on her. Was that a threat? Or supposed to be a comfort? She didn't know. Right now she didn't know anything. It all just felt like a bad dream, but she couldn't wake up, even when she pinched herself in desperation.

He motioned toward the door and her parents departed, arm in arm, as if this whole situation had only shored up their own union. The vicar followed, a troubled expression on his lined face. Kirkwood sighed and then softly closed the door behind them. He didn't turn toward her for a long moment, but leaned there, as if gathering his strength.

When he did face her, they stared at each other wordlessly for what felt like a lifetime. Grief and guilt filled her at his expression. At her knowledge of exactly what had been done to force this man into a future he wanted no more than she did. One she only hoped could be escaped.

"Clarissa," he said softly.

She rushed toward him, hands outstretched. "I cannot apologize strenuously enough. I am so deeply sorry, my lord."

He sighed. "Roderick. If we are to marry, I cannot endure you my lording me."

She blinked. *Roderick.* She supposed she'd known his name. Someone must have said it to or around her at some point. But when she thought of him that way, it felt intimate. To call him that...even more so.

"We cannot marry," she said instead of acknowledging the request.

"And yet we must, thanks to my imprudence."

She bent her head. "Not entirely yours. Mine, as well. And I know you aren't a fool. You see the truth."

He was quiet a moment. "You mean, I suppose, that your parents have sought to force this union."

For a moment she fought for the words. Once she said them and supported what he so clearly suspected, he'd surely hate her. Why wouldn't he? "Y-yes, my lord."

He let out his breath slowly and paced away from her, across to the window that looked out onto the garden. He was silent and she forced herself to be the same. She would bear this.

He turned at last and speared her with his bright green stare. "Was that why you told me to stay away a few days ago? Because you knew their plans?"

"No!" She reached for him once more but this time let her hand fall instead of touching him. "Oh no, I didn't think they'd ever go this far."

He seemed to measure her with that response, but his reaction was neutral. "How far did you think they'd go?"

He was requesting confession and he was owed that, in truth. He was being forced into this far more than she, after all. She'd always known that she wouldn't have a choice in a husband, not truly.

"After the ball, my—my mother suggested that you would be the preferred match for my parents." His lips tightened and she wanted to stop, but forced herself to continue. "Your fortune, your position, all of it was what they've always dreamed of when they thought of my ultimate marriage."

"Never emotions," he asked softly. "Never your heart."

She blinked. "No. They don't care about my heart. They care about raising themselves in Society. I know I'm not supposed to speak ill of them, I am to respect them—"

"They don't respect you," he interrupted.

"Oh." She pondered that. "I suppose they-they don't. But either way, that was what they wanted. I knew they intended to push us together, to try to encourage a match. But I had no idea that they would do what they did today."

"You mean follow me when I followed you. Try to catch us alone, hopefully doing exactly what we were doing or..." His gaze flitted over her briefly and she suddenly felt hot again, like she had when he was kissing her. She pushed that unseemly feeling aside. "Or even more."

She wetted her suddenly dry lips. More. She didn't know much about the *more* that came after kissing. Her mother would tell her, she supposed, now that she would marry.

"Yes," she said. "Even if we hadn't been—been," she dropped her voice, "kissing when they found us."

A little smile tilted the corner of his lips. "Whispering it doesn't change what happened."

She glared at him. There was nothing amusing about any of this. "Well, even if we hadn't been doing that, they likely still would have tried to make our being alone together into an offense that required a marriage."

He nodded. "I thought the same."

"I had no part in arranging this. I promise you."

His jaw was still tight and she found herself wondering if he believed her. Wanting him to believe her. Why, she couldn't really say. They hadn't been friends. More like enemies even at the beginning, and then they'd come to tolerate each other, kissing aside. And yet she didn't want him to tar her with the same brush her parents so richly deserved.

"I didn't want this, my lord." She drew a breath. "Roderick."

His cheek twitched when she used his given name. Somehow it felt right on her tongue, even though she had resisted its use. "No," he said at last. "Before we kissed, you were even telling me you didn't truly want a loveless marriage. It's almost funny." He rubbed a hand over his face. "If it weren't so bloody awful."

"You could refuse," she suggested. "You could walk away."

"If I tried, do you think your parents would then cover up what they saw? That they would pay off the vicar so he wouldn't spread the story and let you go on as before?"

Protect her, he meant. And she knew the answer to that. So did he, judging from his expression. She bent her head. "Well, *I* would make it clear you weren't in the wrong."

"And destroy yourself in the process?" He shook his head. "I'm a rake, not a villain. Or at least I do my best not to be so. And even if I were, I couldn't save myself now."

She blinked. It seemed he was more cognizant of protecting her than her own parents. That he worried about both their well-beings, not just his own. Even after she had judged him ill-mannered. "But—"

"The vicar saw us kissing. Your parents have made it in his best interest to be part of this, evidently. It was a moment we both surrendered to. We kissed. I *think* we both wished to kiss."

She swallowed as heat filled her cheeks. She'd been trying to forget the feel of the kiss. To forget what welled up in her when his mouth was on hers.

"Yes," she admitted. "I don't know what came over me, but when you kissed me, it was what I wanted."

Something flickered in his stare. The same heat that had been there before his mouth found hers a short time before. That heat called to some wanton part of herself that she hadn't fully killed with propriety. One she needed to kill, judging from the trouble she had found through it.

"Most of the time these little lapses don't have repercussions," he said. "We might have found our senses. One of us would have stepped back. We each would have apologized for losing control. And then we could have walked away with a good memory."

She touched her lips despite herself and his nostrils flared.

"But for—" he said, and cut himself off.

"But for their machinations," she said with a sigh.

He nodded. "You don't believe they'd quiet this and based on their uncouth behavior, I agree. So we must marry."

It felt like everything was collapsing. "I want to say no."

"But you realize you can't." His tone was gentle now and he reached out to take her hand.

She stared at his thick fingers encasing hers, thought of how warm he'd been when he held her, how firm his lips had been. Her heart throbbed faster, betraying her in this moment when she should feel nothing but torment. Especially when there was so much regret and even loss in his stare. Loss. Which made her wonder what his hopes had been before he had the misfortune to be dragged to her parents' estate.

"Right now we're both shaken," he said. "This is a shock. But soon we will sit down and we'll discuss the marriage. I think we'll want to make clear what we both want and expect from each other."

That idea was so shocking she rocked back a little. "Oh. I hadn't thought of that."

He nodded. "We may not have had many choices in how this came to be, Clarissa. But we'll have all the choices in how we live it out. Now, let's join them in the hallway."

He released her hand and motioned to the door, but as he reached to let them out, she said, "Roderick?"

He turned back. "Yes?"

"You are being very kind about his. Very gentlemanly whether I deserve that consideration or not. I appreciate it."

He smiled slightly. "I hope I'll eventually live down whatever your first impressions were. And that we'll come to some balance that doesn't include actively despising each other."

Then he opened the door and revealed that her family was in the hallway with the vicar still at their side. Only now they had seemed to call out for others. There was a small crowd gathering. Clarissa's heart sank as she stared at the curious and somewhat judgmental faces.

"And there is the happy couple," her mother cried out.

There was a light applause from the gathered few. Clarissa jerked her stare to Roderick and found his jaw set so hard she feared he'd break his teeth. But he didn't lash out. No, he reached back and took her hand.

"Happy, indeed," he said, and tugged her gently to his side. "I see

Mr. and Mrs. Lockhart have announced the joyful news. Well, how could any of us keep it in until a *more appropriate time?*"

Her father laughed. "Well, there's no use being too worried about appropriate now."

Clarissa turned her head. Great God, what had they said to the others? "We are all a little overwrought," she said. "I hope you will all remain quiet about this…this happy news until we can make the official announcement tonight at the supper."

There were many whispers and nods amongst the gathered crowd and then the handful of people her parents had dragged into this dissipated. Roderick glanced down at her. "I think I had best find your cousin before someone tells him this news before I can."

She nodded. "That might be best. I'll manage…them as best I can." She glanced at her parents.

Roderick squeezed her hand and then strode off. But she was warmed by him regardless. She felt like she had an ally. Whether or not she deserved him.

She pivoted toward her parents. "Did you just destroy my reputation with part of our party?"

"We landed you a husband," her father said, his smile falling. "Better than you have done the last few years, isn't it? You should be thanking me. And I thought that since the gentleman didn't seem that excited to be your bridegroom, that making sure he couldn't wriggle out of it was best."

She shook her head. "Well, you have what you want. Now if you'll excuse me, I think I'll go lie down. We should announce the engagement officially at supper, as I suggested. Until then, *please* don't make this situation worse for him. Or for me."

She staggered away up the hall then, not waiting for their response as she would usually do. She could no longer do that. Not when everything in her world was spinning. Everything in her world had been torn apart and the future looked like a horrible, empty space.

CHAPTER 9

Roderick's hands were shaking as he strode from the house and into the garden. He'd been told that George was outside, taking a break from the other guests, and he needed to find him before he was told this news by someone else. He knew his old friend cared deeply for his cousin and he had no idea how he would respond to this sudden match forced by Roderick's imprudence.

He slowed his steps as the actions of that imprudence flashed into his mind. Clarissa's face upturned, her lovely brown-green eyes locked with his. He thought of how soft her lips had been when he took them, how her fingers had clenched against his back when she let out a soft, needy sigh. He had *liked* kissing her. That shouldn't have been a surprise. He hadn't felt the lightning bolt he'd always believed he'd feel upon meeting "the one", but she was attractive. And yet the power of the desire that kiss had sparked was still startling.

"You look like a storm coming to wreak havoc on this little garden," George said, startling Roderick from his thoughts.

He'd been looking for his friend, but thoughts of Clarissa had wrapped so firmly in his mind that he hadn't even noticed him sitting just ten feet away by a fountain.

He stopped and stared at George. His friend was smiling but the expression slowly fell as he took in Roderick. "What's wrong?"

Roderick swallowed. "I have something to tell you. And I...I think you might hate me when I'm finished."

"That's dire," George said slowly, and got up. "Come, we'll walk together."

Roderick nodded and they fell into step together. He sought words as they paced through the twisting paths of the garden. Finally, he stopped and turned toward his old friend.

"You will hear it soon enough. I doubt your aunt and uncle will control themselves any more than they already have." He shook his head. "I am going to marry Clarissa."

George stared at him for what felt like forever, his brow knitted and his mouth opening and shutting like a fish. "My cousin Clarissa?"

"Christ. Yes." Roderick scrubbed a hand over his face. "Every time I say it, it feels like I'm drowning."

"I think you'd better explain that." George folded his arms, guardedness coming into his eyes. "All of it."

"I saw her hustle off from the gathering earlier this afternoon and I followed."

"Why?"

Well, that was the question, wasn't it? He barely knew the woman, she had disliked him since she first laid eyes on him. He had no connection to her beyond his friendship with her cousin. They owed each other nothing. And yet, when he'd seen her face look so forlorn, seen her on the edge of falling apart, he hadn't been able to stop himself.

"Kirkwood!" George snapped.

He blinked. "I don't know. She appeared upset, I wanted to be gentlemanly."

"Gentlemanly," George repeated. "I see. And then what?"

"I found her in the library and she was crying and I only intended to comfort her, but then we kissed."

George took a step back. "You *kissed* Clarissa?"

"Yes." He sighed, the weight of what came next heavy in so many ways. "Your aunt and uncle, they have designs on her future, as you well know. They played those games out by barging in, with the vicar on their heels, and catching us alone in an at least somewhat compromising position."

George was silent for a long moment and his expression was unreadable. "I knew they were mercenary, but I never thought they'd go so far. God, that is a mess."

"They demanded I should wed her to repair the so-called damage to her reputation." He dragged a hand through his hair. "Fuck, I was such a fool. There isn't a way out of it. Not without damaging her. Probably damaging me."

"You're right." George looked as sick as Roderick felt. "If this is what they want and how far they'd go to get it, they'll destroy everything if they think it will get them what they want. Her. You. *Everything.*"

Roderick shut his eyes. He realized now that he'd not only wanted to reveal the truth in his own way to George, but that he'd hoped his friend could provide him with some palatable escape route. But there was as much surrender to his expression as there had been on Clarissa's.

"What about her?" he asked, softer now. "Clarissa. She declared she wasn't part of their schemes. I want to believe her—I told her I did. But I need to know your thoughts. Do you think she was more involved than she declared?"

"No." There was no hesitation in the answer. "Have I ever told you about the relationship between our families?"

"I don't think it ever mattered until now." Roderick motioned to a gazebo that was a few feet away and they entered the coolness of its shade. He sank into one of the benches set in the middle of the space while George went to look out over the rolling hills of the property.

"Our fathers are brothers, of course," George began. "Hers is far younger than my own, by almost ten years. Uncle Marcus was raised spoilt and the fact that there was little for him to do in the world didn't help. My father would be earl eventually one day, of course, so he was raised with that in mind. The next brother went into the military. Another invested his inheritance very well and has a leisurely life as a gentleman growing tomatoes and attending salons. But Marcus? He took the same inheritance and squandered it. Like it was never-ending. And I suppose he had good reason. While my grandmother lived, his living was always replenished. But when she died...well, my father gave him a final sum and told him he would have to make it last because there would be no more."

Roderick shut his eyes. "Jesus. I assume he was livid."

"I think livid and terrified. He was married by then, of course. They'd spent through my aunt's dowry, as well, and Clarissa had already been born. They tried and tried to have a son, but failed. Sometimes tragically."

"He had no thought to take on a profession? Perhaps the clergy or the military? I know your father. He isn't cruel, I'm sure he would have assisted."

"Oh yes, he would have." George rolled his eyes. "But none of that was good enough for my uncle. He was a gentleman and he scoffed at the idea of being so grubby as to *earn* money. Even said it in front of his fine and decent brothers who did just that. As he became more desperate, the rest of the family distanced themselves all the more."

"Cutting Clarissa off, as well."

"Yes. In fact, she's the only reason we are still linked with them in any way. She has a little money in her coffers, but most of that has been stripped away by the greed of her parents. They became obsessed with matching her well and their grasping behavior probably harmed her more than helped. I suppose that's part of why she leaned into the idea of being entirely proper. Because her parents implied that was why she wasn't matching, yes. But also to counterbalance their outlandish actions."

Roderick thought of Clarissa and her book of comportment. Her vague statements when she was overwhelmed that it was impossible to have moderation. Her wearing of plain white, of never drawing attention to her hair or her pretty face.

"She is as desperate as they are," he murmured.

"And yet she's more clever than both of them put together. And I believe with all my heart that she would never agree to go along with a scheme to trick a man into marriage. She is a victim. I know it even before I speak to her about this travesty."

Roderick sagged slightly in relief. He hadn't realized how much he wanted Clarissa to be true. If he was going to be bound to her for life, likely share children with her, homes, a future...he couldn't bear it if she were a charlatan. Or the kind of person willing to lie to get what she wanted.

"This is a nightmare," Roderick said softly.

George nodded even as he said, "Perhaps it won't be as bad as you fear."

"It...it isn't what I wanted."

Now there was pity that leapt into his friend's eyes. "I know. I know what you wanted. But how likely was it that you would truly meet the love of your life out there in the wide world? That you'd be thunderstruck in an instant?"

"Well, now the chance is exactly zero."

"I'm sorry."

He knew his friend was honest about that. He was sorry. He looked up toward the house, trying to find the window to the library where they'd kissed. Then he sighed. "You and Clarissa are close, I know. Do you have any advice on how to discuss the future with her?"

George seemed to ponder that question a moment. "She is...uncertain. A life being constantly criticized and held up as the savior of the family did that. I would suggest you be gentle with her. The shock of this must be overwhelming to her."

Roderick nodded. "Yes. Gentle. I'll try."

He might have said more, but at that moment there was a great ruckus from the terrace behind them. They both turned toward it and when Roderick squinted he could see Mr. and Mrs. Lockhart standing together on the terrace, gathering the party to them. Clarissa was standing behind them, her appearance ragged and exhausted.

"Christ," Roderick muttered, and started toward the stairs back up to the crowd, George on his heels. He had a sinking feeling he knew what was happening. Yet again without his leave or a thought to how it would look or sound. And that was proven to be true when a sweaty footman met them halfway to the stairs.

"I've been sent to get you, my lord," he panted. "They're making an announcement and want you to join them."

"No," Roderick muttered, and took the stairs two at a time to get to the crowd. He could hear what they were saying now as he rushed to them.

"—though our daughter hasn't had much success, as you well know," Mr. Lockhart was saying.

Clarissa bent her head, Roderick could see her trying to be smaller behind her parents. Trying to disappear.

"Ah, there is Kirkwood!" Mrs. Lockhart called out, waving him over. "And we can share our enormously happy news."

He smoothed his jacket and went to them, doing everything in his power to keep his expression benign when he wanted to grab both of them by the ears and drag them into the house for a scolding. But it was too late for that now. The storm had come. He had to ride it out.

"Lord Kirkwood and our Clarissa have formed a…a bond since he joined us," Mr. Lockhart said. "We've told some of our guests already, but we're pleased to announce to the rest of the party that they'll marry by special license as soon as we return to London in a few days."

There was a gasp amongst the crowd and Roderick felt all their eyes swing on him and Clarissa. He responded by stepping closer to her, resting a hand on the small of her back so she would know he was there. She jumped a little at the familiar touch and then looked up at him. She put on a false smile, but he could see her blinking back tears.

"I am exceedingly happy that the lady has said yes," he managed to croak out. "And cannot wait to call her my countess."

The crowd applauded, though they still looked stunned on the whole. Some of the gentlemen put their heads together to talk and the ladies stared at Clarissa. Her cheeks were dark pink, but she managed to look serene otherwise and unbothered even though he could feel her trembling against his palm.

"Our supper tonight shall be a celebration," Mrs. Lockhart said with a wide smile, as if this was all wonderful. "And our farewell ball tomorrow even more of the same. We'll see you all tonight."

That ended the afternoon event and the guests began to go off in pairs and groups. Some went inside, likely to rest briefly and then ready themselves, others took the stairs to the gardens for walks. George slipped up closer and briefly squeezed Clarissa's hand. She wouldn't look at him, just bowed her head as her cousin stepped away.

"I thought they were finished," she whispered with only the barest glance toward Roderick. "They dragged me down here before I could stop them."

Roderick turned toward them. "You needn't have done that," he growled just under his breath at the Lockharts. "I thought we agreed to wait until supper to share the news with the entire party."

"Now or later, what does it matter?" Mr. Lockhart said with a laugh. "Come now, I had to be certain neither of you would renege on the agreement and now you cannot."

Roderick squeezed his eyes shut and fought with his desire to make a scene. As if George felt that, he rushed to his aunt and uncle. "Why don't we go inside as a family and have a drink before we all take a rest and get ready?"

"I need a moment," Clarissa said so softly Roderick thought he might have been the only one to hear her. She looked up at him, bottom lip trembling. "Please."

He nodded and then stepped away to urge her family inside. "I think that's a wonderful idea. Come then, I'll join you three while Clarissa gets some air."

George took his aunt's arm and herded Clarissa's parents away. Roderick glanced back at her as she walked to the edge of the terrace and clutched her hands along the railing, her head bent. She looked defeated. As defeated as he felt. And though they shared the emotional weight of this day, he realized neither one of them was ready to share it with the other.

Which meant that they were alone, and that was what he feared most going into this marriage.

~

Over the years Clarissa had experienced a few times when her emotions had overwhelmed her. It felt like a fist opening in her chest, pain and worry spreading throughout her body until she shook from head to toe. Now she stood looking out at the garden and battled the war to keep herself from screaming.

Losing herself to this would only be a break in protocol and she needed good comportment more than ever now. This misstep ensured that she would have to walk the straight and narrow path for many years before people would forget her surprise engagement to a man who clearly didn't want her.

"God," she whispered, shaking out her tingling fingers and trying to push those difficult thoughts away so they wouldn't take over.

"Miss Lockhart?"

She stiffened at the sound of the Marquess of Mickenshire's voice at her back. When the engagement had been so suddenly announced, she'd seen him in the gathered crowd and his surprise had been evident. And then he'd glared at her. He hadn't stopped glaring at her during the entire horrible display her utterly proud parents had just concluded.

She turned slowly and hoped her expression was serene. "My lord. I didn't see you there."

"I assume not," he said with a sniff as he looked her up and down like she was something disgusting he'd scraped off his shoe. "You seem to have forgotten me entirely after acting a tease for the last few days."

Her mouth dropped open. She could understand if he were irritated with her, but she hadn't expected him to say it so plainly. She cleared her throat and wished her chest didn't feel so heavy as she tried to find words.

"My deepest apologies, my lord," she began. "Yes, you and I had begun to spend some time together, so I can understand how—how confusing this sudden announcement might have been to you."

"We were on the edge of an official courtship," he said coolly, and his watery stare narrowed on her again. "We *both* know that."

She drew a breath. How did propriety say she respond to this conversation? Did she ignore the truth and soften everything? Did she accept responsibility? Oh, how she wished she could have searched one of her books for some answers that she couldn't find on her own.

"If I had been so—so lucky as to have been courted by you, Lord Mickenshire, I would have been most grateful."

"And yet you are now marrying another. So what was this dance, Miss Lockhart? That is what I wish to know. Were you toying with me only to catch the eye of a rake like Kirkwood? To make him see your value by flaunting your potential attachment to another, one with higher rank?"

Her lips parted. "To do so would have been abominably rude, sir. I assure you—"

"Yes, *abominably*," he interrupted, and stepped toward her. She took a step of her own backward, but she was against the terrace wall now and had nowhere to go. "I'm glad we agree. I do not like to be made a fool, Miss Lockhart."

"Then do not make yourself one."

They both turned at that statement and she caught her breath as Roderick exited the house and strode toward the two of them in long, certain steps. He stopped beside her, ever so subtly blocking her as if offering her…protection. And oddly, she *felt* protected. Relieved that he had intervened.

"I beg your pardon, young pup?" Mickenshire blustered.

"Miss Lockhart was kind enough to share some time with you in the last few days, but there were no agreements, were there?" Roderick asked, holding the other man's stare evenly.

"N-no," Mickenshire admitted.

"You had not asked her to court, nor offered her marriage?"

"Roderick," she said softly.

Both men looked at her briefly and she realized she had called him by his given name and only made this worse. She clamped her mouth shut and forced herself not to intervene a second time.

"I had not. And it seems I am better for it considering all this behavior." Mickenshire smoothed his waistcoat. "I can smell a scandal being covered up from miles away. As can everyone else. So I suppose you have done me a favor, Miss Lockhart, keeping me away from the kind of woman who would—"

Roderick stepped closer to him and pressed a hand to the older man's chest. "Careful now," he said softly but not kindly. "Be very careful."

They stared at each other for a long moment and then Mickenshire turned away. "Good day."

He moved off into the house and only then did Clarissa gasp in a breath that was more like a sob. Roderick turned toward her, his harsh expression for the marquess softening when it fell on her. "Are you well?"

"Not at all," she said, for she had no ability to politely respond. It seemed all propriety was gone now. "Why did you return to the terrace?"

"When I went into the house, I felt like you might need some support," he said. "I suppose you wouldn't want mine, but I wanted to be certain you were well either way. And I'm glad I did, for I overheard that blustering arse beginning to berate you and that couldn't stand."

"He isn't wrong, though," she said softly. "I violated Society's expectations. I behaved without decorum or thought. I should be better than that."

He shook his head. "This obsession with propriety seems not to allow for you to be human."

She blinked. "I don't understand what you mean."

"To feel is human, as is to express those feelings," he said. "That was what you did in the library earlier. To desire comfort is human, and it's what I offered and what you accepted. Even a kiss is human, it's physical connection."

"Spoken as a true rake who may, and presumably *has*, kissed anyone he likes," she said, then lifted her gaze to him. "You do not need to concern yourself with Society's expectations in the same way I do. You are titled, rich, and most importantly, a man. You'll be forgiven for almost anything you do if you're clever enough. While I'll be called a wanton for leaning into a kiss. For being caught in a library in the arms of..." She broke off.

He took a long step toward her and the tension that had been harsh in her chest seemed to ease a little. Or at least change. Changed back into the flutter of excitement she'd felt just before he kissed her. When he was close, that was what she thought of as she stared up and up at him, into those dark green eyes that held such certainty and warmth.

"You may tie yourself in knots, Clarissa, but know this: you didn't harm Mickenshire by any of your behavior. He had no right to be rude to you. That was *his* breech of propriety, not yours."

Her lips parted at that defense of her, but he didn't allow her to respond, he simply continued. "We will marry, there is the truth of it. One of my duties as your future husband is to stand between you and anyone who would dare take advantage of your sweetness. Whether that's a clod like Mickenshire or your parents or anyone else."

She caught her breath. What Roderick was describing was a champion. Had she ever had one of those? Occasionally her cousin had stood up for her, though always playfully, more distracting than defending. But this man had already warned off a potential dragon. He said he would do the same for the rest of her life.

Her eyes stung at the idea. "I...thank you," she said.

He inclined his head and offered her an elbow. "I'll escort you inside. Do you intend to go to your chamber to rest before supper?"

Suddenly she felt the exhaustion of the day. "Yes. I was trying to do just that when they started found me."

"Well, I think they're finished now."

She took his arm and allowed him to lead her inside. He said nothing, just took her to the stairs where he released her. "I'm going to have a drink. I'll see you tonight."

She nodded, mute with surprise at this side of him. He watched her as she went up the stairs, she felt his gaze on her back with every step. And though she didn't look back, she felt the warmth of him even when she was long gone from his company and back at her own door.

She just didn't know what any of it meant. Not for today and certainly not from the future that had been thrust on them both by a slip of propriety and the cruel machinations of her parents.

CHAPTER 10

S upper had gone as well as one could expect with everyone staring and judging. Afterward Roderick stood amongst the gentlemen, sipping a not particularly good port and watching some of the others play billiards. His now-future father-in-law stood across the room, grinning like a fool at some of the other gentlemen, accepting congratulations like he'd just won a prize.

Roderick's stomach turned.

"You look like you could use a stronger drink," the Earl of Ramsbury said as he stepped up beside him. "Or at least one of better quality."

Roderick managed a weak smile. He and Ramsbury had always been friendly. He liked the other earl, with his easy companionship and strong sense of loyalty. He was someone Roderick could be at least partially honest with.

"After Lockhart went on and on about how good the port was, it's evident he poured something far cheaper into an old bottle." Roderick sighed. "All smoke and mirrors, it seems."

Rather like the upcoming marriage. Both Mr. and Mrs. Lockhart had been going on and on about it every time he caught a snippet of their conversation. Bragging and lying and pretending that this was something wonderful when it was really a trap they'd laid.

"Marianne is fond of Clarissa," Ramsbury said carefully. "And my wife has impeccable taste."

Roderick nodded slowly. "She is everything a lady should be," he said and thought of her on the terrace with her pained expression.

"Would it help to talk about it?" Ramsbury asked. "We could step outside for a cigar and likely escape the rest."

"It's a kind offer," Roderick said with a smile for his friend. "And perhaps later I'll take you up on it. But right now I think I prefer brooding over it all."

Ramsbury nodded. "I understand."

"No, you couldn't. I've seen you with Lady Ramsbury. You two are clearly well matched."

Ramsbury's face lit up. "We are. But I think others might not have seen it as possible at the beginning. She was a wallflower, and while I think Clarissa isn't quite that, she is certainly not what one would expect a man like you to match with."

"Yes, she's very concerned with what Society thinks is right. I, on the other hand, have never given a damn." Roderick shrugged.

"And perhaps that will work in your favor. She'll soften your edges, you'll make her braver to be herself." Ramsbury squeezed his shoulder. "If you want to be happy, you can be, I think."

Happy. Oh yes, Roderick wanted to be happy. He'd always pictured what that happiness would entail and saw it as himself head over heels in love with his wife. With an instant attachment that made it clear his choice was correct.

Luckily he didn't have to say anything in response. Mr. Lockhart made the announcement that the gentlemen would rejoin the ladies and they all filed out. Ramsbury stepped away to speak to another gentleman and Roderick filtered himself to the end of the line of men so he could have a moment alone.

When they stepped into the parlor where the women had gathered for sherry and whatever gossip they had shared, Roderick watched

Ramsbury. The earl immediately found his wife and the way her smile blossomed when he approached her was almost blinding in its power. He slipped an arm around her waist, leaned in to say something close to her ear. She blushed a little and laughed, her hand coming up to his chest briefly.

Roderick turned his face. Yes, *that* was what he'd always pictured. That easy affection, brought on by a powerful love that flowed beneath everything. And yet when he found Clarissa at the window, when their eyes met, it was different. Yes, for a moment he had a flash of her upturned face, her trembling lips before he kissed her. Then she turned her head, broke the contact of their gaze.

This was not a love match. It hurt, but he had to accept that. And he had to determine, with her, what that meant for the life they would share. The sooner the better.

Clarissa's body felt bruised, like she'd been in a fight all night, rather than simply sharing supper with people she would call friends and acquaintances. But she'd had to hold herself so straight, had to keep her expression calm when they congratulated her on her upcoming nuptials, had to pretend not to understand when they pried about how this had all happened so swiftly. It had been an exercise in restraint that felt harder and harder to perform. Her back hurt, her arms hurt, her head hurt from all of it.

At last, though, she was alone in her chamber, in her nightrail and dressing gown, her hair down around her shoulders. Any nosy friends who had descended on her at the end of the evening as she tried to simply find her bed were gone. Her maid was gone. Her mother was, blessedly, gone. She could remove all her masks now and simply *be*.

And just as she had that thought there was a knock on her chamber door. Her shoulders hunched and she let out a long sigh. Who was coming to bother her now?

She trudged to the door and opened it. To her shock, it was

Roderick there waiting for her. Her breath became nonexistent as she looked him up and down. He had stripped out of his jacket and rolled his sleeves to his elbows. She stared at the definition of his forearms for a moment, an odd tingle in her body at the sight of his bare skin. She wasn't meant to see that and yet she couldn't look away.

She did just that and jerked her gaze to his face instead. Unfortunately it offered her no respite from inappropriate thoughts. With the dim light from the hallway behind him, he was mostly shadow. Like a fallen angel here to offer temptation. To what, she wasn't certain. But it didn't feel proper.

It was in that moment she realized she was in her dressing gown and tugged it tighter around herself. "You—you shouldn't be here."

He inclined his head. "Likely not. But you and I need to have a conversation, preferably before the wedding that is barreling down upon us, and I doubt we'll be left alone for any length of time until then."

She pursed her lips. He wasn't wrong on either account. Her parents would swoop in with all the protection in the world now to ensure this union happened. "But this is my room. My bedchamber."

"I'm well aware." His voice was suddenly lower, smokier and a ripple went up her spine at the change.

She chose to ignore that feeling even though her cheeks flamed. "Propriety—"

He sighed. "Yes, yes, I know. Propriety. Please let me come in. We're more likely to be caught if I'm standing in the hallway. I promise I have no intention of violating the rules of propriety beyond this one."

Could she trust that? She thought of how he'd put himself between her and the marquess earlier in the day. How gentle he'd been when the machinations of her parents had been revealed. He might be a great many things, but she didn't think Roderick was the kind to force what wasn't invited.

She stepped back and let him into the room. He looked around and her blush deepened, so she closed the door and then hustled past him. Anything to keep her back to him so she wouldn't have to watch him analyze her life through her knickknacks and pictures and books. She could still feel him watching her, though. Almost like he was an inferno at her back.

"I believe in love," he said.

She staggered to face him then, her mouth dropped open in the shock she couldn't hide. "What?"

His face looked pained. "My mother and father, they truly loved each other. And they liked each other. I think they were each other's best friend."

Clarissa shivered at the thought of such a thing. She'd certainly not been raised in that manner. Her parents were scarcely anything to each other. In fact, she sometimes thought they might hate each other at the core of it. But the kind of union Roderick described was bewitching. The stuff of novels, not real life. And yet he said he believed in it.

"How—how did they meet?" she asked, and was surprised that her voice trembled.

His wobbly smile tugged something in her chest. "She entered an assembly in Bath and their eyes met and that was the end for them both. Love at first sight. Amongst their friends, the story was legendary. Told in either hushed tones or with rolled eyes. Either way, their connection was immediate and powerful and they were married within months."

She nodded. "I see."

But she *didn't* see. She'd never imagined such an out-of-control notion before. That one could be stricken by emotion like one was by an illness or an accident.

"I always knew I'd have the same," he continued, and rubbed a hand through his hair. It made the locks stand up here and there, the dishabille he didn't seem to care about so opposite to her own attention to every detail of her dress, hair and way she held herself.

"I see," she repeated softly, for he seemed to be waiting for an answer.

"Yes, I've been what some might call a rake," he admitted. "I haven't lived as a monk, but that wasn't why I haven't married yet. I simply knew that the moment the right woman came along, I would feel an immediate pull to her. A bolt from above that would practically light her from the heavens and let me know she was *the one*."

She realized then what he was saying. Certainly he hadn't felt such a thing with her. They'd barely tolerated each other for days and only declared a truce only for the sake of others. There had been nothing between them until he kissed her so unexpectedly in the library.

"You've lost that," she whispered, and the guilt that accompanied the words was almost unbearable. She moved to her chair before the fire and settled into it to keep her trembling legs from being obvious.

He shifted. "I intended to be honest when I came to you, but I don't wish to be cruel. Still, yes. I've lost the possibility of such a marriage now."

"I am sorry, my lord." She shook her head. "God, you will despise me eventually, won't you?"

"That's the last thing I want, Clarissa." He moved to take the chair that was beside her own and sat on the edge so that his knees were close to hers. "I don't want to hate you or have you hate me."

She examined his face in the firelight. He looked so earnest in this moment. Like he was far more than he pretended to be, certainly more than she'd judged him to be on first sight. "I don't want that either."

"Good. Is that our first agreement?" He smiled a little.

She did the same, despite herself. "*Othello*," she reminded him.

"Oh yes. We couldn't forget *Othello*. Our second agreement then. We're on our way to a happy future, I'm sure." His teasing expression faded. "This will all be rushed. Your parents pushed the idea of the special license to so many people that there will be no choice but for me to obtain one. We'll be back in London within the week and probably married a few days after that."

Her vision swam and she gripped the armrest of the chair with all her might. "Yes," she squeaked out.

His brow wrinkled and his hand came to cover the one on the armrest. When he touched her, she relaxed just a fraction and her breathing slowed a little. "When it's over, though, then it will just be you and me. So *we'll* get to decide what a marriage between us will look like."

She worried her lip. "What do you suggest?"

"Perhaps we could be friends."

Friends. With this man. Truth be told, she did often see his charms. And he was intelligent. He could be kind. Not to mention that in her most secret admissions, things she'd never say out loud, she had very much liked kissing him. The idea of being his friend was not repugnant.

"I would like to be your friend."

He leaned closer again and the half-smile was back, along with the wicked twinkle to his eye. "Even though you think me a scoundrel, Miss Lockhart?"

"Today you weren't a scoundrel at all," she said, refusing to tease back about so serious a subject. "Under the most trying of circumstances, you've been nothing but gentlemanly."

He arched a brow. "Except when I kissed you in the library."

"Yes, thoroughly," she admitted with a blush.

He chuckled. "I could have been more thorough."

She turned her face because she didn't really understand what he meant. He'd touched his tongue to hers, how could one be more thorough than that?

"Did you like it?" he asked.

She refused to look at him and instead picked at a loose thread on the upholstery of the chair. "The kiss? It is unseemly to say."

"Propriety tells you that?"

She did glance at him then, trying to see if he was mocking her. He had a serious expression, though, so she nodded.

"There is only us here. I'm asking for honesty between us. Did you like it?"

When he'd covered her hand earlier, it had calmed her, but now the riotous emotions were back, her breath was short again. He was treading into waters that felt very dangerous and yet there was a thrill in her chest, not fear. Why did she feel that?

"I...I did," she admitted, and then lifted her hands to cover her burning cheeks.

He smiled again. "There is the physical part of marriage, Clarissa. I don't know if your mother has spoken to you about it yet as you haven't been engaged before. But...I do want you. Desire you."

She blinked. "I'm not certain what that means."

He made a little strangled sound in his throat and then got up to pace away from her. "Well, we'll work that out. We'll be friends and I hope lovers. Perhaps that will be enough in the end. I do promise you that I'll never harm you or control you. I'll never make you afraid."

She stared up at him, declaring this vow that felt as powerful as whatever one they'd take in a church so soon. She felt compelled to make one in return. "And I-I'll never embarrass you. I'll do everything to make my duties as countess pleasing to you. To always elevate your legacy with my behavior."

His brow wrinkled a little, but he nodded. "I believe you."

He had moved to stand near her dressing table and he glanced down. She realized he had discovered her copy of *The Mirror of the Graces* and she rose, blushing as he lifted the book and looked at it, thumbing through the pages.

"A comportment manual?" he said, glancing up at her.

"Yes. My mother gave it to me for my birthday. I've been making a study of it the last few months."

He nodded. "I see. Perhaps once we're wed, you'll allow me to review it."

"Why would you wish to?"

"A gentleman must behave well, too, mustn't he? Especially a married one. Perhaps you'll be a good influence."

To her horror, she laughed and he immediately grinned at her response. Lord, but he was handsome when he did so and there was an odd flare of pride in her chest that she had surprised and delighted him in this way.

She stepped back. "Of course, when we're married all I bring to the union will be yours, my lord. The book included."

"Excellent." He set the manual down and walked to the door. There he hesitated and she watched as his gaze fluttered over her. He licked his lips and then swallowed hard before he said, "Goodnight, Clarissa."

"Goodnight, Roderick."

He left her room and shut the door behind himself. She stared at the barrier between them, feeling almost empty. As if something had been left undone between them. What, she couldn't say.

Well, she supposed she could. He'd said he desired her, asked if she'd liked kissing him. Maybe there was a small, very small, part of her that had assumed he would repeat the action. That he would kiss her.

Had she wanted him to kiss her? Propriety be damned? She wished she could say no. And yet that wasn't the truth. So she had to push that down and focus on the promise she'd made to him. If she wanted this marriage to work, she would have to do all in her power to give him no reason to be sorry he'd made it.

Aside from the tragic thought that he'd given up all his dreams of true love for their mistake. And that was something she didn't think she'd ever forget.

CHAPTER 11

The rest of the country party had flown by in a blur. Just as Roderick had suspected they would, Clarissa's parents hadn't allowed for him to spend time alone with her. They were always chaperoned by one or the other of them. Always kept from putting their heads together. He supposed that was to keep them from conspiring to break the engagement.

Now they were back in London, he'd arranged for the special license two days before and tomorrow was the wedding. This was almost over. Everything he'd built his hopes and dreams around was almost over.

He bent his head and stared at the desk in his study, wishing a hole would open up and he could tumble down into it and escape the future. Not because of Clarissa—she was as much a victim as he was—but because he no longer had any agency over what would happen next.

There was a knock at the study door and he straightened. "Enter."

His butler, Stevenson, stepped into the room. "I beg your pardon, my lord. The Earls of Ramsbury and Delacourt have arrived, along with Viscount Lockhart."

Roderick blinked and rose. "Oh. Was I expecting them and forgot amidst the rush?"

"Not that you told me. Would you like me to tell them you aren't in residence?"

"No," Roderick said with a shake of his head. "I'll join them. You needn't announce me, I know the staff is very busy preparing for the wedding gathering tomorrow and the preparation of the new countess's chamber. Where are they?"

"The blue parlor, my lord." Stevenson bowed his way out and Roderick followed a moment later, smoothing his jacket as he made his way to the parlor in question. He stepped inside to find the three men pouring themselves drinks. Ramsbury lifted the bottle of whisky with a grin as he entered.

"One for the groom, as well?" he asked.

Roderick flinched a little at the word, but nodded. "Er, yes. Good evening, Ramsbury. George." The two men nodded in acknowledgment. He looked at the third, the Earl of Delacourt. Another old friend from school. "And Delacourt. I haven't seen you since your marriage. How are you?"

Delacourt inclined his head. "Devastatingly happy, had no idea a person could be so. Though the transition is still awkward."

Roderick frowned. Delacourt's new countess had once been known as Lady Charlotte, daughter of a marquess. She had disappeared right after her father's death and the mystery had kept Society whispering for years. Her reappearance, then swift marriage to Delacourt along with the hanging her father's heir for a litany of crimes, had caused those whispers to grow ever higher. The pair were often accepted, but just as likely to be shunned by those in Society.

He thought of Clarissa and her death-locked grip on propriety. This was why, after all. It was easy to lose standing for things far less impactful than the dramas that had felled Delacourt and his wife.

Not that the man looked felled. He almost glowed with happiness.

"And now you shall join our little club," Delacourt said, and slung and arm around Roderick's shoulders. "George, you must find a bride soon, as well."

George wrinkled his nose. "Great God, no. I shall not marry until I'm in my sixties, and then only to produce the damned heir my eventual title demands."

The others laughed. Ramsbury nudged Delacourt as he handed over the drink. "Sounds familiar."

"We came here for Kirkwood," George said. "Not to harass me."

"For me?" Roderick said and sipped his drink.

"Because you are to be married tomorrow," Ramsbury said. "And there hasn't exactly been celebrating out in the countryside, has there?"

Roderick glanced at George, who shrugged, as if giving him permission to grouse. "No," he said slowly. "Clarissa is as much a victim of this rushed union as I am, but her parents…"

George laughed. "You needn't cut yourself off for me. My aunt and uncle are like cackling crows, cawing out their triumph without a thought to how desperate and pale both the future husband and wife look."

Roderick finished his drink and set the glass down. He thought of Clarissa in her bedchamber, the night they had last been alone. When they'd spoken about what a marriage would look like. He'd been attracted to her then. Wanted to kiss her. Wanted her to want to kiss him. At least there would be that.

He sighed. "Not entirely desperate," he said. "Though I can only speak for myself. Mr. and Mrs. Lockhart were very careful to keep Clarissa and I apart after the engagement."

George pursed his lips. "They do love to cut off their noses despite their faces, those two. They have so little faith in my cousin that they cannot see that if the two of you were allowed to get to know each other better, it would smooth the way for the marriage."

"I suppose we'll have a lifetime to get to know each other after tomorrow." Roderick sighed and poured himself another drink. He didn't want to get drunk. He wanted to be sharp and aware for tomorrow, so he sipped this one more slowly. "I hope we can become friends over time."

Ramsbury wrinkled his brow. "I thought you were the great believer in true love."

"But I'd know by now, certainly," Roderick said.

"It took Marianne and I years to fall in love," Ramsbury said. "Much to the disapproval of this one here." He pointed at Delacourt, who gave a brief, playfully dark look.

"I very much approve of you making my sister happy," he said with a little smile. "As for Esme and I, she certainly wasn't in love with me the moment we met. And I felt desire for her, but I wouldn't have labeled it love."

"And *I* don't believe in love at all." George laughed and threw up his hands. "So I'm not any help. Though I do think if anyone could convince a man to love, it's my dear cousin. Tightly wound as she has been trained to be, she is also the very best of women."

Roderick stared into the amber liquid of his drink. His two married friends, at least, were challenging his idea that love was a lightning bolt, instantaneously felt and understood. They were implying that he could fall in love with Clarissa. It was an odd thought. One that gave his chest the strangest ache.

Still, he wasn't ready to give up the plans, the hopes and dreams he'd spent his life cultivating. Not even to spin up an illusion that would make all of this more palatable.

"Either way," he murmured. "This is happening tomorrow. So I must toast the marriage, toast my future bride, and toast the hope that we'll come to some accord that will keep us content through a long life together."

He lifted his glass and his friends exchanged worried looks, but then did the same. "To Kirkwood and Clarissa," Delacourt said.

They clinked glasses and Roderick downed the rest. If he'd hoped to spend the evening getting some level of calm before the wedding, that had not happened. His mind was only more tangled now. He only hoped Clarissa was having a better time across London.

~

"Tomorrow is your wedding and I believe it is time you and I had a talk."

Clarissa looked up from the letter she had been writing and found her mother had entered the parlor and was worrying her hands at the door. "A talk?" she repeated, rising from the escritoire and coming toward Mrs. Lockhart.

"About…about your wedding night." Her mother blushed dark red.

Clarissa's heart jumped a little. She'd expected her mother to have this conversation with her after any engagement she managed to procure, and here the moment was. Her stomach turned a little.

"Oh," she said. "Well, I see. *The* talk."

Her mother waved her to the settee and took a place beside her. She glared at Clarissa, almost as if she was doing something wrong. "Do you know anything?"

"No, Mama. Few of my friends are married and those that are don't exactly go around talking about their, er, relations with their husbands. I know very little."

She thought for a moment about the way Roderick's mouth had felt against hers when he kissed her. About the heated thrill his touch caused to ricochet through her body. In the library she had wanted more. She didn't know what more was, but she'd still felt this base longing for it. Something she wasn't certain was wrong or right.

"A marriage is meant for procreation," her mother began. "Especially when it comes to a man like Kirkwood, who is titled. He'll want at least an heir and a spare for inheritance. And since women cannot control whether we produce a boy or girl child, that means you may not be able to fulfill your duty with only two pregnancies. Anything can happen."

Clarissa heard the bitterness in her mother's tone and worried her lip. She had long known what a disappointment she had been as the only viable pregnancy her mother had been able to complete. Her parents had wanted more children, boys preferably, but even more girls to marry off. But in the end, it had just been her. Her to place all their hopes and goals and disappointments on.

The weight still felt so heavy.

"I realize that part of my purpose as countess will be to bear children," she said.

"Your main purpose, more than anything else you do. A purpose you may be forced to sacrifice your life for." Her mother shook her head. "It is the only thing of real value you can provide to keep a man interested in you as his wife."

Clarissa flinched at that thought that her intelligence or wit or kindness would hold less or no interest to Roderick. He hadn't seemed to agree with that, but it didn't mean her mother was wrong. Especially since the forced engagement had stolen the very romantic future he'd already admitted to wishing for.

"So you must be open to doing your duty at any time or place your husband requests," her mother continued. "Even if you don't wish it. Even if you don't like it. You just lie there and go somewhere else in your mind and know that you are doing your part in creating a future for your family and your country."

"What exactly *is* my duty, though?" Clarissa asked. "What are you implying I shall lie there and have done to me?"

Her mother got up and poured herself a sherry, which she gulped down with a gasp. "A man and woman must rut, my dear, in order to create children. In that way we are nothing better than animals. Your earl will make his demands. He'll lift your nightrail and then...then he'll unfastened his trousers and put his member in you."

"His member?" Clarissa repeated as her eyes widened. "Oh. You mean..."

"Yes, that thing between his legs. It isn't very nice, but it's necessary. He'll move around and it will pinch and hurt a little. Sometimes more than a little. Finally, he'll be done with it and leave. Once he does, I suggest you lie on your back for a while and lift up your legs to help the miracle of life along. The sooner you complete your duty, the sooner the requests will go away. He'll likely even find someone else to go bother with them. Men have mistresses. It's the way of the world."

Disappointment filled Clarissa at this description. When Roderick had kissed her, it had been so nice. So gentle, and yet it filled her with a sensation she couldn't name. But her mother described what came next as unpleasant.

Plus, the idea that Roderick might find another woman to go to with his desires was a little frightening. What if he felt that powerful explosion of love he expected with another person? What if their marriage became entirely empty while he shared everything else with a mistress who he actually cared for?

"And that's that," her mother said, and smiled. As if she'd just given Clarissa good news. "Has your father talked to you about your marriage contract?"

Clarissa almost laughed. "I assure you, Father has discussed nothing with me. Why?"

"Well, your Kirkwood has been very generous with his agreement regarding your monthly pin money. He seems to be as rich as we had hoped. You should send as much of that to us as you can. Three-quarters of it."

Clarissa blinked. "You wish me to give you most of my pin money?"

"Well, we're paying a dowry and that has stripped a great deal of funds."

"I see."

She didn't. She had actually been aware of how much that dowry was. A measly five hundred pounds and a little house on the edge of her grandfather's estate that was run down. That miserly sum was probably part of why she'd struggled to find a husband. Men married for money. At least in her world.

"We have sacrificed all our lives for you, Clarissa." Her mother's voice was sharp now. "You will send the funds along to help us. And encourage your husband to support us with additional funds, as well."

Clarissa swallowed. All her books reminded her that she was never to refuse her parents. To do so would be impertinent. So she nodded even though she resented the demand so very deeply. It seemed they would take everything from her in the end, even the pleasures she could choose for herself from her pin money.

Her mother drew a sharp breath to continue when their butler, Boulton, stepped up from the hallway. "Mrs. Lockhart, Miss Lockhart has visitors. The Countesses of Ramsbury and Delacourt."

Her mother pivoted first to Boulton and then back to Clarissa. "You see? An important marriage has its benefits. Though…Lady Delacourt." She pulled a face. "A scandal there. But still. Let them in. Of course, we wish to see them."

Clarissa rose, still smarting from the conversation with her mother and tried to force a serene expression as Marianne and Lady Delacourt entered the room. Clarissa couldn't help but draw a sharp breath. Lady Delacourt was truly stunning, with thick red hair and the clearest blue eyes she'd ever seen. Both women wore brightly colored gowns of expensive silk and for a moment Clarissa felt drab in her simple white gown and light brown pelisse.

"Mrs. Lockhart, Clarissa," Lady Ramsbury said as she and Lady Delacourt gave little nods to both of them. "I know we weren't expected, but I hope we are still welcome."

"Of course," Mrs. Lockhart said, and smiled at Lady Ramsbury but sniffed at Lady Delacourt. "What a delightful honor to see you both."

Clarissa's cheeks grew heated at her mother's subtle dismissal of Lady Delacourt, but the countess didn't seem to mind. She gave a little smirk and then smiled broadly at Clarissa.

"Miss Lockhart," she said as she came across the room with hands outstretched. "How happy I am to hear about your marriage. I wish you the greatest felicitations."

"Thank you, Lady Delacourt."

"We came in the hopes we could help the bride pass a few hours," Marianne said to Mrs. Lockhart. "I know I was dreadfully nervous the night before my marriage. Perhaps we could steal her away in the parlor and giggle like schoolgirls for one last time."

Mrs. Lockhart's smile fell as it was made very gently but also firmly clear that she was not invited to this event. She pursed her lips. "What a lovely idea. I'm sure my daughter would appreciate it. I'll leave you then."

She gave a quick curtsey and exited the room. Marianne shut the door behind her and then crossed to where Lady Delacourt was still standing with Clarissa. "*Is* it appreciated?" she asked gently. "Esme and I would never intrude if it weren't. I don't want your mother to speak for you."

"Somehow I sense she knows you very little at all," Lady Delacourt added softly.

Clarissa glanced at the two countesses. She had become very fond of Marianne at the country party. There was nothing but kindness to her. And she and Lady Delacourt shared the sting of a scandal, even if hers was far less shocking than the return of a missing lady from who knew where.

"I think a little time with friends would be wonderful," she said. "Thank you for coming, Marianne. My lady."

"Esme," Lady Delacourt insisted. "If we are to be friends, I must be called Esme."

Clarissa nodded. She'd learned from Marianne that there was no use arguing against such a request. And she supposed that tomorrow she would join the ranks of the countesses of Society. So it wasn't so deep a breach. At least that was what she told herself. "May I call for tea or pour some sherry?"

"Let me," Esme said. "You are pale as paper. Make her sit, Marianne."

Marianne took her arm and led her to the settee as Esme went to the sideboard and dug around in the bottles there looking for something for them to drink.

"I felt as though we interrupted something with your mother," Marianne said. "I'm not sure if I should apologize for that or not."

"I'll thank you for it," Clarissa said, and smiled up at Esme as she handed her a crystal class with a splash of sherry. Esme sat in the chair across from the settee and leaned forward. She was very focused in her attention, as if every word Clarissa said was important.

"Ah, so it wasn't a pleasant conversation." Marianne squeezed her hands. "I'm sorry, my dear."

"And now you've gone from pale to red as a tomato," Esme said. "Which makes me think I know exactly what your mother was discussing with you."

Marianne's eyes went wide. "Oh. Is that true? She was having *the talk* with you?"

Clarissa squirmed. Ladies didn't talk about such things. Well, that wasn't entirely true. She knew the married ladies sometimes discussed private matters. Discreetly. But they always stopped talking when the unmarried women entered the room.

"I'm embarrassed to admit it," Clarissa said. "But…yes, she was."

"And you look sick," Marianne said slowly.

"How could I not be when someone speaks of such horrors?"

"Horrors?" Esme repeated with a quick glance toward Marianne. "Oh dear. That sounds terrifying. And wrong."

"Wrong?" Clarissa repeated and her cheeks had never felt so hot in her entire life. "Oh. She would know, though, wouldn't she?"

"It depends," Marianne said gently. "I know there are some ladies who don't like what happens in their bedchambers. And there are some who very, very much do."

That was encouraging at least. Clarissa shifted and bit her lip as she looked from one woman to the other. She had seen the connection between Marianne and Lord Ramsbury—it was impossible *not* to see it whenever they were near each other. She'd also heard that Esme and Lord Delacourt had also married for love. Shocking, passionate love.

"Would you like to tell us what she said?" Esme encouraged, her expression softening. "And then we can…we could correct her if we feel she isn't right."

"Or at least tell you if there are other opinions," Marianne added.

Clarissa's chest felt tight and it was hard to draw breath. Everything in her books would scream at her to never, ever say such things to her friends. But in that moment her need to have solace and support overrode propriety. She had to say this out loud to someone. Had to calm the fears her mother had put into her.

She glanced at the door as if her mother would come raging into the chamber, and then told the two women what had been described to her. Both of their expressions grew increasingly horrified with every word. And Clarissa became more and more embarrassed. She was utterly relieved when she finished and bent her head. "So that is all."

"That poor woman," Esme muttered, and slugged back her sherry in one gulp.

"Esme," Marianne said softly, but she also finished her drink and handed the empty glass to her sister-in-law to refill as she took Clarissa's hands. "I think *anyone* would be nervous if they were told such things about what happens between a man and woman. That doesn't sound nice at all. But it also doesn't have to be accurate."

Clarissa shifted. "It doesn't?"

"No!" Esme burst out as she turned back with the full glasses. "Lord, no."

Marianne pursed her lips at Esme. "Gracious, my dear, let's be gentle about this."

Esme set her glass down and held her hands up as if in surrender. "My delightful and kind and wonderful sister-in-law is far better at gentle, while I am perhaps known in our family to be more direct. I think there's value to both. Which variety of opinion would you like first?"

"Perhaps we start with direct?" Clarissa said slowly. "After all, my mother could return to interrupt us at any moment."

Esme looked triumphant at that and Marianne let out a little laugh. "Yes, you've won. Go ahead. Though I'm not sure I should listen, as you are married to my brother."

"You can cover your ears if it becomes too much," Esme said with a little wink. "Now, Clarissa, I suppose the physicality of what your mother told you is correct. Technically a man will put his cock—"

"Esme!" Marianne seemed horrified at the word, which made Clarissa blush even hotter.

"What? That's what it's called. *You* learned it, she should know it, too."

Marianne glared at her sister-in-law but it seemed to be playful. "One should never tell you secrets. Go ahead, though. You cannot be stopped, I know."

"A cock," Clarissa said weakly. "That's what he calls his member."

Esme nodded. "Yes. He'll put that inside of you and yes, he'll—" She sighed heavily and rolled her eyes. "Move around, as she put it. And eventually he'll spend, which is what she meant when she said it would be over. The result of that could be a child. But other than the technicalities, your mother is full of shite. Horse shite, to be more specific."

Despite herself, Clarissa laughed. Then she covered her mouth. "Oh, I shouldn't laugh at that."

Marianne put an arm around her. "In this instance, you are safe to do so. You're amongst friends. You needn't worry about our impressions or reactions."

"I actually like you more for laughing," Esme said. "If that helps."

Clarissa drew a long breath. "Very well, tell me where she has it wrong. If it isn't the horror that she described, what *is* it like?"

"Do you understand what a rake is known for?" Marianne asked.

"I suppose for behaving wildly. For being linked to women, many women." She shivered at that thought.

"Yes. And the reason he can connect with all those women is because he is very good at, er, relations," Marianne said gently. "Women wouldn't fall into his arms if he were so rote and unfeeling about his partners. I obviously don't know Lord Kirkwood beyond his friendship with my brother and my husband. But if he is anything like them, if he earned his reputation as they both did, one would assume he also has skill. That he would take care with a partner and ensure her pleasure before he thought of his own."

"Her pleasure would be part of his pleasure," Esme murmured, and there was a light that came into her face when she said it. "It is intoxicating, really."

Clarissa squeezed her eyes shut. Her mind was being bombarded with all kinds of opposing thoughts. Reminders that ladies did not speak of such things, images of Roderick's handsome face close to hers before he kissed her. She felt caged now, trapped by everything she didn't know, everything she thought she knew, everything she wanted and hated herself for.

"Will you truly not judge me?" she asked, hardly able to get her voice above a whisper.

"Never in your lifetime or ours," Esme replied instantly. There was a kindness to her gentle tone. Something that said she had endured and now held strength and understanding for anyone who needed it. Clarissa clung to that strength with all her might.

"He...Roderick...Kirkwood...kissed me in the library," she said slowly, for she hadn't told anyone this truth yet. "*That* was why we were forced to marry. We were caught by my parents and our vicar and they insisted there must be a reckoning."

Marianne shook her head. "I wondered."

"And even though there were so many terrible consequences for it, when he kissed me I-I liked it. I felt things. Like I was warm all over, like I tingled in places that made me blush."

"*That* is desire, my dear," Esme said, and smiled softly. "When Kirkwood touches you on your wedding night, when he readies you for the parts your mother so inadequately described, you'll feel that desire grow. Multiply. And then all you'll want is for him to do more."

Marianne nodded. "It's true. Yes, there's a little nervousness about doing something that feels so strange, something we women have been trained to fear and avoid. But it can be wonderful. Something that bonds you together, something you'll find yourself craving whenever you look at him and see that certain gleam in his eye. Passion is something I think every woman should experience."

Clarissa's body flexed at that idea, almost against her will. Again, she was torn between two seemingly opposing truths: that she should shun such things, but that she could want them. Should want them.

"Says the former very innocent wallflower," Esme teased gently, and startled Clarissa from her thoughts with those words. "So you know she's right."

Clarissa smiled at them. "You have made me feel better. I hope your version of my wedding night and any night beyond it will be the true one."

Marianne nodded. "As do I. I recommend, though, that you speak to him about how you feel. I'm sure he'll guess you're nervous, but the more you communicate, the easier the entire thing will be."

Though that made perfect sense, Clarissa shifted. Talk to Roderick about all this? That seemed impossible. He was just too…too big and certain and…and male. They were still on shifting sands, even though they had declared they could be friends. Discussing something so intimate with someone barely more than a stranger felt wrong somehow. A breaking of those rules that pressed down on her at present.

"I'll try," she promised, and then shook her head. "We shouldn't talk about this anymore. You've been so kind already. But why don't we just pretend that I'm not getting married tomorrow and we're just friends gathered to talk about normal things? Tell me some gossip, hopefully not about myself, or inform me where to buy the best hats. Anything but this."

Esme laughed. "I think we can do that."

"Absolutely," Marianne agreed, and then the two of them launched into conversations meant to distract and soothe her.

She appreciated it enormously and it did help. But she couldn't help but still think about Roderick, her wedding in less than twenty-four hours, and what would happen afterward that would change their relationship forever. She just hoped she would be ready for it.

CHAPTER 12

R oderick hadn't known what to expect during his wedding. He'd actually be avoiding thoughts of the ceremony all together. But when the doors to the chapel opened at nine a.m. and Clarissa stepped in on the arm of her father, his heart almost stopped.

She was wearing a beautiful gown. White, of course, because she never wore anything but white, it seemed. It cascaded over her curves, the bodice covered with lace and champagne frills. Her hair was done to frame her face, her very pale face, he noticed as she came closer and closer. Her lovely face.

This wasn't what he'd dreamed of, but in that moment, he wasn't upset or angry or disappointed. There was no room for any thoughts but of her. When her father reached them and extended her hand to Roderick, he took it, squeezing gently to offer her comfort. In that moment, her expression softened, her smile became more genuine and she squeezed back.

They faced the vicar, happily not the one from the country estate who had interrupted their kiss, but the one from Roderick's London parish. The man droned away about the purpose for marriage, the goodness of fruitfulness. Roderick didn't pay attention to any of it, he just watched Clarissa's face, noting every little twitch and blush. Every blink that lowered her long lashes over those lovely brown eyes with the hidden green he couldn't stop searching for.

She said the words the vicar required. He did the same and then it was over. They were declared man and wife at last and turned toward the crowd of gathered family. Well, her family. He had so little family left. Her mother and father were beaming, obviously smug that their plans had worked. George was there, of course, his expression a little troubled, though he smiled at Clarissa as if to encourage her.

Roderick guided her down the aisle, outside where a few friends waited to throw flower petals and strangers waited for him to throw the coins that would bring luck to the union. Since he needed all he could find, he did so, watching as the children scrambled to collect them.

Then he helped Clarissa into his carriage and followed, the church bells fading behind them as they rolled off across town to his home. *Their* home, he supposed now. The one she hadn't even seen yet, due to the odd insistence of her parents to keep them separated before they wed.

She worried the hem of her glove a little and then glanced up at him. "I'm sorry," she said.

His brow wrinkled. Was that truly going to be their first interaction as man and wife? He didn't want it to be. Didn't want her first memory as his countess to be one laced with guilt. But since he had no idea what to say to her in that moment when she looked so utterly beautiful and so fully broken, he instead leaned across the distance between them, gently cupped her cheeks and did what he'd been dreaming of for almost ten days.

He kissed her.

C larissa hadn't been expecting the kiss, but now that it was happening she was yanked back to the first time he'd truly kissed her in the library. To all the desire, that was what her friends said it was, that had risen up in her. It returned immediately now, making her hands shake, and her stomach flip. She rested her palms against his chest, gripping at the lapels of his fine jacket for purchase and leaned in closer.

He made a soft sound from his throat and then his mouth opened, his tongue tracing hers gently. It was almost a question, a request to let him in. She did and tasted minty freshness on his breath, felt the rough stroke of his tongue against hers that suddenly made the carriage too hot and close.

This was what Marianne and Esme had spoken to her about. These flutters and heated aches. They would only grow, become more intense, make her ready for whatever he would do to claim her as his wife. She shivered at the thought and he drew away with a heavy-lidded expression.

"You are so beautiful, Clarissa," he said softly, and gently tucked a lock of hair behind her ear.

She shivered again at the intimacy of that featherlight touch. "Th-thank you. And you are very handsome."

He smiled a little. "Was that painful to admit?"

She laughed and suddenly the tension bled away. Strange that he could do it so easily. "No, my lord," she chuckled.

"Good, *my lady.*"

She blinked. "Oh my, I suppose people *will* address me as such now, won't they?"

He laughed again. "Yes, because you are a countess. My countess, if you want to be specific about it."

"I think specificity is a must in these circumstances," she teased back. She stared at her hands then, still resting on his chest. She drew them away and worried them in her lap. "I-I hope I'll be good at it."

His brow knitted and he moved to her side of the carriage slowly. She slid over to offer him space and he put his arm around her. A comfort, though she never would have pictured she would appreciate it so much when she'd first met him and told herself to despise him for being unmannerly. In this moment, all he was was gentlemanly. Kind.

"You will be, Clarissa. I've no doubt of that." He sighed and tucked her a little closer to him. "I wish your parents had allowed you to visit my home earlier, because we'll have to have a truncated introduction to the servants before our guests arrive for the wedding gathering."

She worried her lip. "I believe they feared that if you spent too much time with me before the marriage, you might change your mind."

He stared at her. She fought not to show her hurt at that fact. Her parents had said it more than once. She'd overheard it and also had it stated directly to her face. In truth, she had feared it could be true, considering what he'd confessed about true love when they were in her bed chamber in the countryside.

He touched her chin and gently turned her face toward his. "Christ, I thought they just didn't want us making a united front against them. If they actually said such a horrid to you, I want to disabuse you of that notion. I *never* would have changed my mind. There is nothing you could have done or said that would have made me do so. You'll find I'm a man of my word, whatever my other faults are."

She swallowed hard. With his face so close to hers, all she could think about was kissing him. Lordy, one wedding and she was a wanton, forgetting all propriety.

"I believe you, I think," she said.

He laughed. "You think. I'll take that. Oh, we're approaching the estate now." He pulled the curtain away from the carriage window and together they leaned toward it so she could see the beautiful home coming into view as a black gate opened to allow them entry.

"Oh, Roderick," she breathed. "It's wonderful."

He said nothing, but was beaming at the compliment that was entirely meant. It truly was a glorious mansion, almost sparkling white in the autumn sunshine, its massive stone front supported by tall, beautifully carved pillars. Slightly behind the grand entrance she could see the hint of a rounded roof.

"There's a rotunda?" she breathed.

He nodded. "Yes. As well as a beautiful garden and a library in that very rotunda that is to die for."

"Better and better! I cannot wait to see it all," she gasped, and grabbed his hand with both of hers briefly before she blushed and released him. "My apologies. I'm clearly overwrought."

His brow wrinkled. "You shouldn't apologize for having a reaction to your new home. If you had been staid and unfeeling, I would have been nervous."

The carriage had stopped by now and the servants came down to open the door. Roderick gave her one last smile and exited first, then reached back to help her down himself. When she was safely on the ground, staring up in wonder at how much more beautiful the home was with every look, he tucked her hand into the crook of his arm and led her to the front door where a line of servants waited for them.

She tensed. What they all must think of her when everything had been so sudden and rushed. But they were smiling and as Roderick swiftly introduced her to them, they all gave little bows or curtsies.

"And this is my butler, Stevenson. Stevenson, may I present the Countess of Kirkwood."

"My lady," Stevenson said and gave a low bow. "How happy we are to greet you at last."

She stepped forward. "I'm very pleased to be here, Stevenson. What a wonderful home you and your staff have kept. I cannot wait for you and his lordship to give me the full tour."

The butler smiled broadly and it softened his stern face. "I will be pleased to do so, my lady, and give you all the history of the place that you can bear. Perhaps tomorrow?"

She nodded. "Oh yes! I very much look forward to it."

"All is ready, my lord." He said to Roderick.

"Thank you, Stevenson. The throng should be shortly behind us.

I'll take the countess to her chambers in case she needs a moment and we'll join the others shortly."

"Very good." Stevenson stepped away and Clarissa looked up at Roderick.

"Ready?" he asked softly.

She hesitated. "Not exactly, but I'll follow your lead."

Something lit up in his gaze and for a moment she forgot her breath. But he said nothing and simply guided her down the long hallway, past rooms she had to fight not to look into, and then up a winding stair into the next level of the house. A turn to the end of one side of the hallway and there was a great double door, walnut in color and beautifully carved and offset. He released her, turned the brass handle and stepped back to allow her to enter the chamber first.

The antechamber made her catch her breath with its dark blue hues on the walls and in the fabric that covered a lovely sitting room set. There was a large window along the back wall and she crossed to it, her hands shaking as she looked down on the most beautiful garden she'd ever seen in the city.

"Oh, it's lovely," she whispered.

He moved toward her. She felt it rather than dared to look. "It truly is. I love my...*our* country estate but I'm so pleased that we have such a large garden here so I don't always feel walled into the city. It's worth the little drive back into Town proper."

She nodded. "It is, I can tell already."

"Would you like to see your chamber?" he asked.

She turned to face him and couldn't help but think of the night he'd come to her bedroom in her parents' home. Now they'd be alone in a bedroom again, but this time they were married. It felt a little fraught with tension, that idea.

"Clarissa?"

She blinked and then forced herself to nod. "Y-Yes," she whispered.

He moved toward one of the doors on either side of the antechamber and opened it. Again, he let her go first and when she did, she clutched her hands to her chest. While the antechamber was done in dark blues, rich hues of midnight, the countess's chamber was done in pale versions of the same colors. The wallpaper was warm gold tones and cerulean depths in a shell pattern, the bed had a darker version of the same blue in its fine coverlet and curtain hangings. A soft rug that covered most of the wood floor was spun in a beautiful repeating butterfly pattern with dark, medium and light blue mixed with pale yellow and dark pink.

"Oh, it's…"

"Blue," Roderick said with a laugh. "It's very blue. I never changed it—my mother was very fond of the color. You may, of course, alter it however you see fit so that it suits you. Something to discuss with Stevenson tomorrow or in the weeks to come, if you'd like."

She turned toward him and shook her head. "It's very kind of you, but I think it's beautiful. Your mother had impeccable taste."

There was a brief sadness that filled his eyes. "She did, yes."

She found herself moving toward him, a desire to comfort him filling her. She wanted to know more about the woman who had raised him. About her loving marriage and his loss. She blinked and pushed that aside.

"Er," she murmured and rubbed her hands together. "I'm not sure what to do now."

"We don't have long," he said and shifted his weight. Then he smiled. "I'll be honest with you, Clarissa, I'm also at a loss."

"You are? And you admit it?"

He laughed. "Well, neither of us has ever been married before, have we? I don't think either of us has any better notion than the other. We have a little time before we join the party for the gathering. I can hear them all starting to arrive."

She was quiet for a moment and in the distance she did hear the sound of faint voices, of doors closing and opening.

"I could show you my room," he said. "Or if you'd like a moment alone, there's plenty of time for that later."

His gaze flitted over her when he said that and her legs went a little weak. His bedroom. Would that be where they consummated this sudden union? Or would it be here in this pretty bed? If she followed him, would he try to get that over with now? He kept looking at her and when he'd kissed her in the carriage he'd seemed to desire her.

"Perhaps a moment wouldn't be the worst thing."

He inclined his head and she could sense no disappointment in his behavior. "I'll come back for you in a few moments, then." He backed from her chamber and closed the door behind himself.

She sucked in a shaky breath and moved to the dressing room on the other side of the chamber. Her maid had been coming and going for a day or so and her gowns and other things were already arranged in the room. There was a pretty dressing table with her brushes and combs laid out. That made the place feel like home, at least.

She returned to the bedroom and walked to the bed. She touched the coverlet and found it to be soft as silk. Her fist bunched against it and she shut her eyes.

She was the Countess of Kirkwood. Roderick's wife. That was forever. And somehow she had to come to grips with that fact before the party so she could behave correctly. Come to grips with it before they returned to this chamber later tonight and the full union of their lives was made.

She just wasn't certain how.

Roderick hadn't wanted this marriage, and yet when Clarissa shakily asked for a few moments alone, he'd been a little disappointed. Oh, he understood. Like him, she had to be overwhelmed by the turn of events of the last few weeks. But still, when she stood in her new bedchamber, looking at him with those wide, beautiful eyes, he had wanted to touch her. Not take her, perhaps, but kiss her again, certainly. Lie down beside her and let his hands begin an exploration that they could finish at their leisure later.

But he couldn't push. For both their sakes. And so now he stood in his own bedchamber, staring out the window as their guests milled about the garden with its changing autumn colors. He glanced at the clock on his mantel and sighed.

He crossed back over to her door and hesitated before he garnered the courage to knock. "Come in," she said softly.

He opened the door and found she was just coming down off the bed, as if she'd lain down for a moment on it to gather herself. There was something so intimate about seeing her like that. Not sexual, though he supposed there was that about seeing his new bride slithering off the high edge of the bed, but intimate on a deeper level.

"It's time," he said.

She moved to the mirror mounted above the fireplace and checked herself, smoothing her gown and her hair before she turned toward him. "Am I presentable as Lady Kirkwood?"

"You would be in sackcloth," he assured her as he offered her his arm.

She blushed and he reveled in that as he took her from the room and back downstairs to the ballroom at the back of the house. This wasn't a ball, but it was a big enough chamber to hold a great number of friends and gawkers who would bless this union while eating his food and drinking his spirits. All the doors along the back of the huge room were thrown open, allowing guests to pass in and out of the room onto the terrace behind the house.

She drew in a harsh breath as they entered. "Oh, it's lovely," she whispered. "The ceiling, Roderick."

He glanced up. He'd always lived in this house and her joy at discovering it made him truly look at it. The ceiling was a delight with its decorative plaster flowers and duel pale purple and light blue paint. There were a few Greek-style reliefs on the ceiling, as well, with sprites pouring water from urns and gentlemen in togas eating grapes from trays.

"Lord and Lady Kirkwood," his butler announced to the gathered crowd.

Clarissa jumped at that declaration and looked at him briefly as the guests began to applaud and bow to them. He watched her uncertainty fade then, replaced by all the ways she had been trained in propriety over the years. Things he'd scoffed at, but immediately he began to see their value.

For the next few hours, he couldn't take his eyes from her. Once they parted ways, she moved from group to group with an unpracticed ease, talking to friends and family without hesitation. She truly engaged with those around her, listening intently when they spoke, leaving them smiling when she departed them.

She was kind to his servants, as well, but still held to her position as their mistress. She addressed small problems and kept ahead of anything that could become one. Her role seemed to settle on her shoulders without trouble.

He could feel her reading the room when she was alone for a moment, seeking out anyone who was shuttled off against the wall or looking uncomfortable. She always brought those people in, helping them find the perfect company to join with. It was truly a revelation to observe and drew his attention away from those he spoke to more than once.

She turned toward him and for a moment her gaze rolled over him from head to toe. She swallowed hard and he found himself doing the same. He shifted with the desire that filled him, stronger now that he'd been watching her, seeing her in this new light. His wife. Someone whose partnership would make him all the stronger. He hoped he could do the same for her.

"Ah, look at the besotted groom."

Roderick shook his head and turned toward his in-laws as Mr. and Mrs. Lockhart approached him. He'd only spoken to them briefly during the gathering thus far and had managed to avoid them otherwise. But now they stood grinning like ghouls.

"It seems we made a very good match for you both after all," Mrs. Lockhart said.

Roderick set his jaw and thought of what Clarissa had said earlier about her parents fearing he would change his mind if he spent time with her. It had clearly hurt her and it was patently untrue. This little time together today had given him a bit more acceptance of the circumstances.

"Anyone who matched with your daughter would have been the luckiest of men," Roderick said, lifting his chin and leaning into the protectiveness that filled every pore of his body.

"Very good," Mr. Lockhart said, and barely glanced in his daughter's direction. "It doesn't matter anyway, you cannot give her back now, even if you wished to do so."

Mrs. Lockhart laughed like that was a good joke.

"I do not wish to do so, sir," Roderick said quietly. "I vowed to take care of her and I shall. From *anyone* who ever threatens her peace, physical or otherwise."

"And her family, one hopes, eh?" Lockhart kept smiling, but there was a mercenary light to his gaze.

Roderick arched a brow. "The provisions we agreed to will be fulfilled. Is this truly what you wish to talk about on your daughter's wedding day? You do not wish to celebrate her? Or discuss your hopes for her happiness?"

Mrs. Lockhart blinked like he'd spoken another language, but then nodded. "Of course, of course. I'm sure you will make her very happy. Look at this house! How could anyone be anything but happy here?"

Roderick shook his head. He knew full well a person could be here and be very unhappy. Grief or broken heartedness didn't spare someone based on the fineness of their walls. But he was beginning to see, more plainly than ever, that his wife's parents had only ever truly cared about their own comfort first.

Something that made his stomach turn.

"It seems the party is beginning to break up," he said, and motioned toward the guests who were milling around the ballroom exit. "I must collect Clarissa for our goodbyes."

He inclined his head and moved toward her, watching her catch a little breath as he reached her and smiled. "Will you join me in the first farewells?"

She nodded and slid her hand through his arm. Her fingers squeezed his bicep and a thrill of sensation followed in their wake. Soon enough she would touch him and there would be no barriers between them. An intoxicating thought that made him want to clear the room with as much haste as possible.

Still, he managed to rein himself in and continue the task of host. There was plenty of time for everything else soon enough. And he was very much looking forward to it.

CHAPTER 13

Clarissa smiled as she watched her husband help Lady Nance, one of Society's oldest ladies, into her carriage. He was so gentle in the way he did so, so kind in how he spoke to her and bade her farewell. He could be, and often was, so entirely gentlemanly. Not just because it was expected, but because it was who he actually was. She had misjudged him before and she was glad of it.

At last that carriage departed, though, and he turned back to her. They were alone now. All the guests gone with their well wishes still ringing in the rooms around them. He'd even managed to get her parents off with little trouble.

"You were wonderful, my lady," he said softly. "Your first act as countess can be called nothing but a great success. I was told I am the luckiest of men by at least a dozen partygoers."

"Oh. That's very kind." She bent her head. He didn't truly believe he was the luckiest of men. She knew what he'd wanted from life. What he'd lost by being forced to be married to her.

"Are you tired?" he asked.

"I am." She glanced up at him.

"There will be time to...to rest before supper. It will be late tonight."

"Rest," she repeated. "Are you also going to rest?"

He nodded. "I'm going to go upstairs. I can take you."

She looked up at him and was caught up in the dark intensity of his eyes. How she wished she knew him better to know what he was thinking. It was impossible when all he did was take her hand and didn't speak further as they returned to the chamber at the top of the stairs. In the antechamber they stopped. She turned to face him.

He was watching her intently. She swallowed hard. "Will you show me your room now?"

"I...I don't want to rush you, Clarissa."

Rush her. She supposed that was kind. But it made her worry that perhaps he didn't want her as much as he had before. That the shine was off the diamond even before they'd begun. The fear loosened her lips.

"You don't want to"—her cheeks felt like they were on fire—"to consummate the union?"

"Oh no, I most definitely want to consummate this union." He took both her hands and lifted them to his lips, kissing both sets of knuckles one after the other and sending shockwaves of sensation through her. "But this has been a long day. We're both still adjusting to all the changes. And I don't want you to feel obligated to come to my bed. I want you to do it only when you are ready."

"You really are a gentleman," she said softly.

He smiled. "Not as much as I should be."

She let that sink in a moment. He was giving her the space to be ready. But he was also putting the onus to drive this part of the marriage onto her. To make the decision rather than be swept away. She sighed. "I'd like to see your chamber, Roderick. I'd like to do the things a married couple is meant to do, because I'm so nervous about them that I fear I'll make them into something terrifying if I wait too long. But also because..."

She trailed off and he voice was breathy when he said, "Because?"

"Trust you to make me say it," she muttered. "Because every time you kiss me I feel this pressure all over my body. I've been told by friends that it's desire. That it's the wanting for what we'll do in that chamber. I...I want this."

He moved forward a step and touched her cheek, gliding his fingertips down to her jawline. She leaned into his touch, her eyelids fluttering shut as she gave a shaky sigh. She heard his breath catch, then he leaned in, bent his head and let his lips brush hers gently. She lifted into him, meeting him as she had in the carriage. Now she couldn't contain a little moan..

"Come then," he murmured, drawing her across the room toward his chamber. "I won't make either of us wait anymore."

Clarissa shook as he drew her into his chamber, his mouth finding hers over and over as he guided her. When they'd stepped inside, he released her and let her step forward and look around while he locked the door behind them to insure privacy.

The other room was blue but this one was done in dark greens, highlighted with lighter colors. The ceiling had a crisscrossed pattern of exposed beams and in the ceiling space created within were different painted scenes, some sweetly innocent and some a little more risqué with couples kissing most passionately.

"My father's version of the chamber matched hers," he explained, answering her questions before she could even voice them. "I made it my own."

"It's beautiful," she said, and let her eyes find the bed across the room. It was bigger than the one in the countess's chamber, with heavy dark green bedclothes and bunches of comfortable-looking pillows.

"*You* are beautiful," he murmured, and stepped behind her, putting his arms around her and drawing her back against his chest. She shivered at the heat of him there, the strength of his body cradling her own. How could one feel nervous *and* safe at the same time? They were opposite sensations, weren't they? "You said your friends told you about desire. Did anyone explain what will happen tonight?"

She nodded and then sucked in a breath as he kissed the spot between her hairline and the neckline of her gown. "My mother tried and only made it sound horrible. But then Marianne and Esme came and explained it better."

He shook his head without parting his lips from her skin. "It's like they want to make the marriage as much work as it can be."

"My parents?"

"Yes." Slowly he turned her to face him and she stared up into those dark eyes that now held her captive. "I'm going to do everything in my power to make sure tonight is filled with only pleasure."

He bent his head to hers again and she leaned into his kiss. It was so funny because when he'd first kissed her she'd been so taken off guard, but now she craved the firm pressure of his mouth on hers. She longed for the taste and tease of him as he let his tongue touch hers and turned her bones to liquid. She was spiraling into the pleasure of just that when she realized he had begun to unfasten her gown.

She gasped and drew back to stare at him. "You're...you're undressing me."

He smiled a little. "Being undressed is a requirement. Well, for some it isn't, but I much prefer it."

She looked down at herself. He'd already opened three buttons and her dress gaped, revealing the pretty chemise beneath. Slowly, she lifted her hands and covered herself. "No one has seen me naked save a few female servants."

He nodded. "You're nervous. Would you prefer if I go first?"

Her eyes widened. She hadn't thought of that. Him naked for her? "I-I've never seen a man naked either."

She waited for him to become annoyed that she was drawing this out, denying him at every turn, but his expression never gave her that impression. "We'll go slowly. And if you want me to stop, stop anything, all you need do is say so. What we are going to do to consummate this union should be only a pleasure to us both. If it becomes something else, I don't want that."

Slowly, she nodded and then stepped back. "You go first, then."

He shrugged out of his jacket and then unfastened his waistcoat. When he was only in his linen shirt and trousers, he stepped closer. "Will you untie my cravat while I work on the cufflinks?"

Her heart was pumping blood so loudly in her ears that she could hardly hear him. He wanted her to undress him. Strip away whatever pretense of propriety he wore in public. She shivered and found her hands lifting even though she didn't think she'd decided they should. She touched his cravat and felt around for the tucked ends that would allow her to loosen the knot. When her fingers brushed his skin beneath the wrapping, he hissed in a breath softly.

"I'm sorry, did I scratch you?" She pulled her hands away.

"That wasn't a sound of pain, I assure you. I like when you touch me," he said. He had one cufflink free and was working on the other. He stopped and kissed her yet again. "Please continue."

Her hands shook as she went back to her work. She somehow managed to get the careful knot in the fabric untied and then slowly began to unloop the long length of the neckcloth away. He was so much taller than her that it was a challenge, but she found herself laughing went he bent down playfully so she could draw the cravat away at last.

"There we are," he said, and his arms came around her. "This doesn't have to be wrought with worry and tension, Clarissa.

"I beg to differ, my lord," she said, her laughter fading into a smile. "I'm afraid I'll be tense until this is over."

"Not if I do my job right," he muttered, and then he stripped his shirt open and tugged it over his head.

She stared despite the fact that she'd been trained never to do so. How could she not? She'd never seen a man half-naked and here was her husband, a powerful specimen of lean muscle and strength all but towering over her. Again, she was struck by the dichotomy of her emotions. She felt overwhelmed, but the room was also somehow dreamy. Like this was some foggy fantasy.

"I can't tell if you're horrified or thrilled," he said, and the teasing in his tone shook her from her shocking thoughts.

"I—I—both?"

"Oh dear," he said, and came closer. He caught her hand and pressed it to his chest, flattening her palm against the plane of muscle covered in warm flesh. "What is horrifying? Just my face?"

"You know you have a very handsome face," she managed to croak out as she watched her fingers flex against him, felt his body ripple in response. "I just don't know what to think or do."

"You're doing fine," he murmured. "Touching me is exactly what you should be doing. May I remove your dress?"

She blinked. He had gone first, after all. That had been their bargain. This was his right and the longer she waited for it to happen, the more frightening it became. She nodded. "Yes."

Once again he turned her back to him and she felt his fingers go back to the buttons along her spine. His hands brushed her skin as he flicked one after another free and then pushed her dress slightly forward so it gaped down around her chest without falling off her arms.

He moved her to face him again. His pupils were dilated now, his breath harsher. Almost as if he were as anxious about this as she was. But how could that be? He'd had lovers before, she had to be just another in a string of women he took to his bed.

"Breathe," he whispered as he drew her gown down inch by inch, over her elbows, down over her wrists, around her waist and finally pushed it into a pool at her feet.

She had never been on display like this. Not with her chemise brushing mid-thigh and her garters on display and her chest shockingly bare so that one could see the cleavage of her bosom. She raised a hand to cover herself, but it was woefully inadequate.

"Better than I imagined," he said.

She tilted her head. "You imagined me like this?"

He nodded. "Since we kissed in the library and I knew you would be my wife, I have definitely imagined this moment."

She wrinkled her brow. "But you didn't want this. You don't want me."

"I very much want you," he said, and cupped her bare shoulder with his palm. She shivered at the warmth on her skin and the way he dragged his hand down, catching his fingers in the strap of her chemise and tugging it to her elbow.

He moved in to kiss her again and she relaxed a little at that familiar touch in the midst of the warring reactions to new sensations. He deepened the kiss, pulling her closer, letting her body mold to his skin, be closer than ever before. As her riotous thoughts faded, she found herself clinging to him, lifting to him. Wanting him to do more, even if she feared what more would be.

She flattened her hands against his chest and pushed back. He released her immediately and watched as she paced away to the fire. She stared into the flames, trying to ground herself further.

"Too much?" he asked when she'd been silent for what felt like forever.

"I don't know," she admitted. "I've been raised all my life, told by guardians and books and friends and governesses that I'm not to feel such strong reactions, emotions. And yet now I'm supposed to take off my clothes and let you do these things to me that turn me on my head. How can I be both demure and filled with desire?"

His expression changed. She wasn't sure what he felt, but she braced herself for a scolding or to be made fun of. Instead he caught her hand. "Why can't you just be *you*, Clarissa? In this room, in my arms, in my bed, could you forget comportment and propriety and ladylike behavior and just be you?"

She blinked up at him and a horrible fact became clear. "I'm not sure who *I* am."

"You are challenging," he said, and lifted her wrist to his lips to brush them there. She shivered at the cascade of tingles that seemed to flow through her at that touch. "You are intelligent." He kissed her again. "You are kind, regardless of someone's position." Once more, he brushed his lips to her, but this time he moved up her forearm. "You are sweet." He growled deep in his throat and when he kissed the inside of her elbow, his tongue darting out. "Almost impossibly sweet. And you are my wife. So I ask you to trust me. Let me guide you tonight, teach you what this thing you fear and worry and think about over and over can be. Trust me."

Trust him. In truth, she still barely knew him. And yet she did trust him. When she looked up into those dark green eyes, she saw a man who wouldn't hurt her, not on purpose. Perhaps not ever. Such a strange thing to know down to her bones.

"Yes," she whispered. "I-I trust you."

He cupped her face, fanning his fingers along her jawline as she tilted up to offer her lips. He took then and she felt the shift. The kiss was still gentle, yes, but she felt a deeper hunger behind it. A more powerful need that swept over her like a wave in the ocean. Fighting it would be no good. She just needed to float.

So she did, not drawing away when he walked her toward his bed, his mouth still on hers. He caught the chemise strap he'd left at her elbow and drew it all the way down, then repeated the action with the other. When he pushed the fabric away, she was naked for him and she squeezed her eyes shut when he pulled back to look at her.

"So perfect," he murmured, his voice hypnotic and seductive. His fingers pressed into her lower back, bowing her a little, and then she felt his mouth on her nipple.

Her eyes flew open and she stared, watching him lick her, swirling his tongue around and around the tip that she had never known could be so sensitive. When he nipped and sucked her, it sent electric waves of pleasure between her legs, making her throb in time to his touch. She let out a ragged moan and heat suffused her cheeks.

"I-I'm sorry," she whispered.

He lifted his head from her breast. "For what?"

"I don't seem to be able to control my response," she said.

He shook his head and then surprised her by catching her by the waist and lifting her onto the high edge of the bed. They were face to face now, equal in height.

"I want you to lose all control of your response," he said, his eyes locked with hers in the most fascinating way. "Forget everything else, forget whatever you were told or feared. I want to hear you moan for me, Clarissa. I want to hear your breath catch. I want to know what pleases you by the way you rise beneath my tongue and rake your fingers across my back."

She shivered. His words were so wicked and she found herself wanting to lean into him, rub herself against him as he said them.

"The rules of engagement in bed are my expertise," he whispered with a little smirk.

She laughed a little. "I suppose that's true, isn't it?"

"Now lie back," he said, pressing a hand to her shoulders.

She wanted to argue. Who in the world lay back across the bed, their legs dangling off the edge? What would be the purpose? She fought the urge. As he'd said, he was the expert. If she wanted to learn the proper way to engage with her husband in their martial bed, this was the way to study, even if relinquishing control was more than a little frightening.

She rested back, drawing a few long breaths to settle herself, and squeezed her eyes shut. He let out a little laugh and then she felt him move away from her. She opened her eyes and sat up on her elbows.

"Where are you going?" she asked, hating that her voice sounded so desperate.

"Just to get a place to sit," he assured her, and pointed to one of the chairs by the fire before he dragged it across the fancy carpet and placed it where he'd been standing before her naked body.

He didn't take that seat yet, though. Instead, he placed one hand on each of her calves. She shivered at the intimate touch. Men didn't even see a lady's legs, let alone touch them. And here he was with his warm palms cupping her before they began to slide upward.

"Oh," she gasped as he pressed his palms to her knees, let his fingers tickle the sensitive place behind them. He moved higher still and she stopped breathing entirely as she watched his fingers press into the flesh of her thigh right below her stocking. He unlaced the garter and rolled one stocking down, removed her slipper and then did the same on her other leg.

And now she was utterly, entirely naked. Naked with a man. This man. Her husband. Her mind spun with that wild notion and she flopped back and closed her eyes again so she didn't become entirely overwhelmed.

As if he sensed that shift in her, her stilled his hands on her thighs and merely stroked there. "Clarissa?"

She opened one eye and found him watching her. She nodded.

"I'm going to tell you what I intend to do," he said. "I don't want you to be surprised."

"Yes," she managed to gasp out.

"I'm going to kiss you," he said, and then motioned between her legs. "There."

"Why?" she burst out, and sat back up on her elbows again.

"Because it will feel good to you. It will most definitely feel good to me. And it will help ready you for what will happen afterward. The wetter you are, the easier the way, especially this first time." He stroked his fingers against her thigh and she gasped at the sensations that seemed to flow through her whole body.

"Yes," she murmured again.

A flare of response rippled over his face. Something dark and sensual that hooded his gaze as his fingers stroked a little more firmly. "Lie back. And feel," he whispered.

She did so once again and stared at the ceiling above her. She heard him taking his place in the chair, moving around and then his hands were back on her thighs. He pushed them wider and she blushed so hot that she felt she would combust. He was looking at her in the most intimate way possible.

And then his mouth touched her and all rational thought fled. He kissed her inner thigh, slight scratchiness of stubble abrading the tender flesh in the most intriguing, arousing way. His tongue brushed the same place, soothing and making her ache all at once. He licked and kissed higher, higher as his hands pushed her even wider. Then she felt his breath on her sex. She gripped the coverlet in both fists, bracing for the impact she knew was coming but didn't understand.

And when he did as he'd promised, when his mouth covered her in that place she'd been told was wicked or dirty or to remain untouched, she recognized her world would truly never be the same.

CHAPTER 14

Just as he and Clarissa had discussed, Roderick had been with a great many women over the years. But he had never in his entire life been so hard as he was, perched on the edge of a chair between his new wife's soft thighs. Her breath kept catching and little gasps and moans kept escaping her lovely lips, ones he wasn't even certain she realized she was making. It was all intoxicating, as was her earthy scent and the hint of wetness that already existed between her legs just from what they'd done before he put her on his bed.

He wanted to make this woman come. To unravel all her harsh and fearful grip on propriety and see what she looked like when she arched and moaned and shook with pleasure. He couldn't wait.

He pressed her sex open with his thumbs, gently massaging her outer lips. Her legs shook a little when he did, gripping against his arms. He smiled and leaned in to lick her, at first gently, just a featherlight touch to test her flavor. She was sweet and salty, perfect. When he licked again, it was more firm, tasting her entire length as she rose up beneath him with a gasp.

"Roderick?" she murmured, a question, a plea.

He licked again and answered without lifting his head from her body. "That's just right, angel. You're doing just right."

She moaned again, like the praise put her on edge as much as the touch. He marked that, stored it away so that he knew all the things that gave her pleasure, from the very erotic to the seemingly benign. He licked again and again, taking his time with her, judging all her reactions, feeling when she became wetter. She dropped one hand against his head, her fingers tangling in his hair. The little tug of that drove him wild and he moaned against her body.

"Oh!" she gasped, and lifted to him.

He smiled against her. She was beginning to lose control, to roll with the pleasure the way she'd been built to do. Recognizing a dance that couldn't be taught, only experienced. He drew her through it, slowing, drawing his attention to the ripe nub of her clitoris. He smoothed the hood away with his thumb and teased her with the tip of his tongue, then moved away. Back and forth, spending more time there with each sweep until it was all he focused on. He stroked and sucked, gripping her thighs as she began to shake beneath him, on the edge but not quite over.

His heart was throbbing, his cock, too, as she got closer and closer to the edge, lost more and more of the respectability she wore as a shield to the world. This Clarissa would be only his, always his. That thought made him ache and he sucked her even harder as she came in a burst of wetness and flavor on his tongue. He wanted to do this forever, keep her in this state forever. His. Only his.

And he was too aroused to fully examine what that meant or how his world had changed with this first intimate joining that would only connect them more.

Clarissa had felt hints of the pleasure that now ripped through her body, causing her to rise and twitch beneath Roderick's hands and tongue. But this was something else. This was a torrent, an uncontrollable downpour of sensation that broke her into pieces. She thrashed beneath him, trying to find purchase, but he didn't set her free. He drew every drop of pleasure from her until she was weak on the bed, panting with exertion and wonder.

Only then did he rise from between her legs and lean over her, caging her in with strong arms on either side of her head as he kissed her. She tasted herself on his tongue and lifted beneath him against her own will.

He chuckled against her lips. "That was remarkable."

Her world was still spinning, but she nodded. "Y-Yes."

He kissed her, this time on the corner of her lips, nibbling down to her jawline as she gasped beneath him. "Move onto the pillows, please," he whispered.

It took her a moment to understand what he'd said, her mind still addled by the unexpected pleasure of what he'd already done. But slowly, she did as he'd asked and lay there, watching as he unfastened the fall front of his trousers and slowly lowered it.

She stared. There it was, the much talked about member. Cock, wasn't that what Esme and Marianne had said? His cock. He would fit that into her. Suddenly she was nervous again. His tongue had felt full inside of her when he'd been licking her and that thing was certainly bigger than a tongue.

"Er," she murmured.

He shook his head. "Your body was built to accommodate, I assure you," he said. "And we'll go very slowly so that it will." She pursed her lips, both nervous and excited about that idea. He kissed her forehead. "I promise."

There was a strange sensation that rushed through her, as foreign as the pleasure he'd created with his tongue. She couldn't name it, but there was comfort to those words. And this was what was required in a marriage, to consummate the union they'd created.

He joined her on the bed, kneeling between her knees, which pushed them open again. He covered her gently, holding his full weight away with his arms as he kissed her and kissed her and kissed her until all there was was that. All there was was him. Only then did he maneuver himself. She felt the tip of him against her sex as he stroked it back and forth. Just as when he did that with his tongue, there was pleasure.

She lifted beneath him, burying her head against his bare shoulder as her fingers dug into his skin.

"Good?" he whispered.

She nodded without lifting her head and her voice was muffled when she said, "Yes."

"Breathe," he said, and then she felt the tip of him pressing more firmly.

To her surprise, her body did open for him. He slipped in just a fraction and the sensation was powerful. A joining unlike any she had experienced and she realized with a start that this was something she would likely only experience with him. Something secret they shared that bound them. She lifted with the pleasure of that thought and took him a little farther.

The pressure increased in kind and she felt the faint tingle of pain mixed with the satisfaction of his claiming. She must have tensed without realizing it for he lifted his head and looked at her.

"I know," he whispered. "Slowly now. You're so perfect."

He'd said that when he licked her and that praise had been as arousing as his mouth. How could that be possible? Her body flexed and he growled out a curse softly.

"My God, Clarissa," he murmured. "You will drive me wild."

Drive him wild. There was a thought. Odd that she felt desperate to see it when a lack of control was usually so frightening to her. But taking his? Oh, that was something else.

"More," she whispered.

His eyes went wide and he obliged, sliding farther. The pain was fading now as she stretched to take his thick length. A little more and he was fully seated inside of her. He groaned her name and rested his forehead to hers.

"So good," he whispered.

She nodded. "Y-yes."

"I'm going to move," he said. "If you're ready."

"I'm ready," she promised, though she wasn't entirely certain that was true. This was all so overpowering and magical and mystical. How could anyone be ready?

He withdrew a little and thrust back into her gently and all the wondering vanished because it felt like heaven. He did it again and she found herself rising to meet him, matching his motion with the grip of her body.

"Yes," he hissed out, and then there was nothing but the roll of his hips against hers, their moans matching in the quiet of the room, the soft sounds of their bodies joining.

Every thrust rubbed just right, building the sensation she'd felt with his mouth all over again. She found herself reaching for it, trying to find it in the dark. His pace was increasing now and the power of this increased with it. Her legs began to shake, she couldn't find her breath, pleasure inched up and up, overtaking everything else but him and she let out a cry she couldn't have held back for any amount of gold in the country.

His thrusts increased, as if the ripple of her body as she gripped him stole more of that control she so desperately wanted. His hands cupped her harder, his breath merged with hers in deep pants as he kissed her. And then he grunted her name and she felt the flood of his release fill her gripping sheath as he collapsed over her, pressing kisses to her throat and shoulders like he couldn't get enough of her taste or feel, even though the deed was done. Their marriage was fully real, in name and in act.

There was no going back. And she found for the first time since her parents had forced both their hands, that she didn't *want* to go back. She wanted to be just where she was.

How long they lie like that, legs and bodies tangled, Clarissa couldn't have said. It felt like a lifetime as Roderick gently kissed her skin, stroked her body with his hands. At last, though, he rolled to the side, propping himself up on one elbow as he stared down into her face.

"Was I too rough?" he asked.

She blinked up at him, wondering at the concern on his face. He was truly worried about her, focused on her experience. How many people in her life had been like that?

"Not at all," she assured him as she reached up to trace the line of his jaw absently.

"Good," he breathed in what felt like true relief. "As much as we tease about my so-called prowess, I will admit I've never taken a virgin to my bed before. I wanted it to be a good experience for you."

She shook her head. "I suppose I hadn't thought of it that way. Your lovers were all…experienced."

He nodded. "This seems a poor topic to discuss with your wife."

She shrugged. "I know you have a past. It doesn't trouble me."

It didn't, that was true. What did trouble her, a little burn in the back of her pleasure-addled mind, was that he might have a future with lovers, too. A love, even. She pushed that thought away.

"Did I disappoint you, though?" she asked. "Since you are more accustomed to ladies with experience in what to do?"

"No," he said swiftly. "God, no. What we just did was uncommonly wonderful. To unwrap the sensuality you hide beneath all those layers of propriety was an honor I'm glad to have."

She worried her lip. "Yes, propriety," she repeated, and dropped her hand from his face as she stared away from him and toward the crackling fire. "Certainly I didn't show much of that while I was writhing naked in your arms. Nor do I feel much of it now when I want—"

She cut herself off, her cheeks burning.

"What do you want?" he asked, his voice low and dangerous again. Seductive, she realized.

She glanced at him. "I want more," she admitted. "I have no idea if that's right or wrong."

"How you feel can never be wrong," he said.

She laughed. "*That* is not true. Not for a lady, certainly not for a countess."

He appeared troubled by that answer. "Well, I want *this* lady, *my* countess, to like it when I touch her. I want you to crave this, Clarissa. It's the most natural thing in the world. I want to feel your pleasure, to know every note of it. And I want you to learn mine."

She shifted. Learn his pleasure. Give him powerful sensations like he had so easily given them to her. Demure and proper or not, that sounded wonderful. Overpowering. Changing.

"But for now," he said gently. "As much as I'd like to slide you beneath me and make your legs shake again, I want to give your body time to recover. Later you can have a hot bath, which should ease you. But there's plenty of time for more, my lady. In fact, I promise you that if nothing else. More and more and more."

He kissed her as he trailed off and she wrapped her arms around him, pushing away any thoughts, any worries, any confusion about what was right or wrong. About what the stirrings in her chest meant for this union Roderick had never wanted.

He drew away and then tucked her into his body, her back to his chest, his arms warm around her. "Rest now, though. You've more than earned it."

He kissed the side of her neck and she shut her eyes, surrendering to his suggestion. But as she slipped into sleep, she couldn't help but wonder what her life would look like now. And how she could define herself as countess, lady...as wife to a man who awoke things in her she hadn't even known her possible.

And made her doubt all the ways she'd seen herself before him.

CHAPTER 15

The first week of Roderick's marriage had not gone the way he expected. Honestly, as often as he'd thought of meeting the love of his life, how he would immediately recognize her as the match of his heart, he hadn't thought much past that. Marriage had been a foggy notion to him.

The reality of it was *interesting*. That was the best word for it. Everything about it was new, unexpected, as he began the slow process of learning the woman who was now his wife.

At the moment, Clarissa sat to his left at the breakfast table, going through invitations and household notes, a cup of tea gripped carefully in her fingertips. She had sunk easily into her role as countess. She already knew every servant's name and at least a little about their circumstances. She was firm but kind in her dealings, always perfectly walking the delicate line between herself and those that served her.

She kept to a rigid schedule. He had learned it almost by heart now. She rose at the same time each day, even if he tried to drag her back into their bed with kisses and pleasure. She readied herself, she answered correspondence, she met with Stevenson for a daily breakdown of what was happening in the household.

Afterward she shared breakfast with Roderick and he watched her just as he was doing now, her still focused on everything but him.

The shell of her propriety existed, even though sometimes he could coax her into his arms in the afternoon, or draw her there at night and strip all that away as he introduced her to more and more pleasure. He was addicted to her at present. To her taste and the way her hair felt when it brushed his skin. To the music of her moans and the tremble of her body when she came.

He shifted in discomfort as his body ached for her, and cleared his throat. She lifted her gaze to his with a little smile.

"What are your plans today, Roderick?" she asked, setting her papers away and focusing all her attention on him. That was another bewitching thing about her. When someone spoke to her, she truly listened.

He winked at her, trying to clear the tension in his body with playful teasing. "I wondered if I might first tempt my lovely wife back to bed."

She shook her head with a laugh. "I am dressed and ready for my day, my lord."

"Oh yes, I know how you hate to be mussed," he said, and took her hand, lifting it to his lips.

She shivered, so he knew she wasn't immune to him. But the propriety was a wall she built. He shouldn't care about that. This was no love match and surely the passion would fade at some point. And yet he wished she would let him past that wall. Let him in further than just her body.

He cleared his throat. "Mr. Brightly is in Town."

"Ah, yes, your estate manager for Stratford Manor in Kirkwood," she said.

He smiled a little. She did recall every detail. "Yes. We'll travel to the estate in a few weeks, so I'll be speaking to him about readying the place and also regarding a few repairs and upgrades that need to be in place before the colder months."

She nodded. "Yes, I believe the almanac predicted a more bitter winter in Kirkwood this year." She worried her lip. "I ought to think about what I can do for our tenants to ensure their comfort. Perhaps prepare baskets when I do my first tour of the estate."

He stared at her, taken in for a moment by her easy kindness. Her concern for people she hadn't even met yet. "That's a lovely idea, Clarissa."

"Are you meeting with Mr. Brightly here?" she asked.

"Yes, at two. Will you join us?"

She sighed. "Oh dear. I'm to meet with my seamstress at the same time."

"You're buying new gowns?" he asked, almost hopeful. She did look lovely in everything she wore, but he longed to see her in any color but white. It felt so bland to him, so bereft of the personality he was beginning to see more and more.

She pursed her lips briefly, clearly troubled, though he wasn't certain why. "One new gown and a fresh lining on a favorite coat."

"What color will the gown be?" he asked, trying not to appear too interested.

She took a sip of tea and watched him over the rim. "White, of course."

He frowned. "Have you ever considered buying a fabric of another color?"

There was a flash of a moment where he thought he saw longing in her eyes. The desire for more than she so often pushed away out of some strange attachment to the idea of doing what was "right". Then it was gone.

"A lady should wear white," she said softly. "And not put too much stock in the cut or color of her gown. The lady should be elegant, not the clothing."

He wrinkled his brow. "You recite that like it comes from a book."

She shifted a little. "And what if it does?"

He raised his hands at the defensiveness of her tone. "I only made the observation."

She rose from the table and so he did the same out of the politeness that she so treasured. "You needn't worry yourself about such frivolous things as my gowns, my lord. You surely have more pressing matters to occupy your time."

"I like considering your gowns." He stepped toward her and took her hand. "I like the idea of you having something pretty that you enjoy."

Her lips pursed and she gently tugged her hand free. "A lady ought not trouble her mind with such things."

He sighed. Once again, there was the wall. Insurmountable at present. Perhaps forever. Why did that make his chest ache?

"Well, I ought to take care of a few things before I make my way to my appointment," she said. "Oh, and my parents will be joining us for supper."

He barely managed not to pull a face. "Very good. Then I suppose I won't see you until then?"

She nodded. "Good day, Roderick."

She moved as if to walk past him, but he caught her arm gently and pulled her back. She stared up into his eyes, the flutter of her swallow the only indication that he moved her. But he saw it. He chased it.

"I'd like a farewell kiss," he said softly.

She made a little sound in her throat, lifting her lips toward him as he lowered his own to meet her. The kiss was gentle at first, but in a moment the heat began to take over. To his joy, she allowed it, opening to him, gripping at his jacket with her fists. But before he could sweep her away, she gasped and stepped back. Her pupils were dilated with desire, her hands trembled a little at her sides as she fisted them there.

"I—" she murmured, and then she bent her head. "Good day."

With that she slipped from the room, leaving him to watch after her and wish, from someplace he didn't fully understand, that he could bring her back to him. Keep her with him. Protect her from the monsters that had caused her to build those walls.

Even though that wasn't his place. He had declared from the

beginning that it couldn't be, and she seemed to agree. So that was that.

~

Miss Swanlea was well known as one of the best seamstresses in all of London. Not only did she have access to the most beautiful and fine fabrics, but she could make a gown that perfectly fit the body of any client. Normally, Clarissa was thrilled to be with the lady, to explore her textiles and discuss what simple cuts of a gown would best display both modesty and timeless style.

But today she was distracted. She kept losing track of the conversation while the seamstress measured her. And worse, now that she was in the showroom to choose the fabrics for her purchases, her eyes kept moving away from the white silks and linens toward the stacks of rainbow colors on other tables spread across Miss Swanlea's small showroom.

"Lady Kirkwood?"

Clarissa blinked. That was her title. She started and looked at the seamstress. "Oh, my apologies," she said. "I seem to be woolgathering. It's so impolite."

Miss Swanlea looked at her a moment. "I notice you keep glancing toward that table of pinks. Would you like to try a fabric with color for this new gown?"

The word *yes* screamed through Clarissa's mind in an instant, overriding all else. She frowned. It seemed her new role as countess was having a negative effect on her. She was only thinking of what she wanted, not what was best or most proper. Perhaps that was what happened when one started craving pleasure like she did now. Pleasure with Roderick.

"I…" She trailed off and looked toward the table again. She moved toward it, almost against her will, and let her fingers drift over a pink jacquard silk. The little flowers that were part of the fabric pattern felt so lovely. What would Roderick say it she came downstairs in this?

"That color would be perfect against your skin," Miss Swanlea said, almost gently, as if talking to a scared filly.

Clarissa released the silk and turned back toward the whites. "All your fabric is perfection. But I believe I must stick to the tried and true, rather than draw attention to myself through fashion. The white muslin for the gown, please. And the new lining we already discussed."

There was a moment where the seamstress appeared disappointed, but she nodded. "Of course, my lady. I'll be sure to have them ready as soon as possible."

"Good day," Clarissa said, and inclined her head when the woman bowed to her. That was truly going to take some getting used to.

She turned and found her maid, Hester, already waiting at the door. They departed together and Clarissa sighed as she looked down the lane. A few doors down was Mattigan's bookshop, one of her favorite haunts. She knew Roderick was busy with his meeting with the estate manager, so she had time to browse.

"Let's go to Mattigan's," she said, and together they walked to the shop.

After she was greeted by the kind and friendly owner, himself, Clarissa took a deep breath and relaxed into the atmosphere of the shop. Tall shelves were arranged in never-ending rows all the way back to the cozy fireplace with its comfortable chairs at the back of the shop.

As Hester stepped away, Clarissa began to walk the aisles, touching the spines of the books gently. There were so many she wished to read, but since she had agreed to give a large portion of her pin money to her parents, she had to be frugal. At any rate, she hadn't fully explored Roderick's beautiful library yet. Oh, how she loved that room with its high round ceiling and bright light from what felt like innumerable windows. She needed to determine if any of her desired titles were already there.

She made a mental note of the titles she needed to search for as she found her way to the Shakespeare section of the shop. There were many different volumes and productions of the Bard's extensive work and she picked almost every one up to look at the different foils and bindings of them. She had almost finished in the section when she noticed a volume of *Othello*. She smiled as she thought of one of her first conversations with Roderick back at her family estate. How they had somehow bonded over *Othello* even in the midst of their early rivalry.

The binding was particularly beautiful on this edition, with gold filigree on the cover and the same on the edges of the pages. She had already looked at all Roderick's Shakespeare volumes and she knew he didn't have this particular version. He would love it, she was certain. She'd always liked finding the perfect gift for people she cared about.

Cared about. Yes, she cared about Roderick. That was allowed, wasn't it, in a marriage of convenience? They were supposed to be friends, after all. Sharing a bed made that more complicated in ways she hadn't expected. The longing she felt whenever he was near her was often confusing. Despite that, she was trying to remain true to their original agreement to what this marriage would look like.

She clutched the book to her chest and went to the raised desk where Mr. Mattigan stood, going through a pile of books.

"Good afternoon, my lady," he said. "I see you've found something there."

"Yes, this is a beautiful version of *Othello*."

"Ah yes, a wonderful printing from Bandy and Sons. They make fine versions of any book or play."

"I'd like to know the price, if you don't mind," she said, and handed it up to him.

"That one is two pounds, my lady," he said.

She blinked. Two pounds! That was an enormous sum, though she should have guessed it. Books were expensive as it was and this one was a beautiful version. Her pin money was generous, but she knew a great portion of it had already been bled away to her parents' account. This would take the remainder of her funds for the month, when she took into account the gown and lining she'd already agreed to at Miss Swanlea's. So much for any other frivolities.

But she thought of Roderick again. Thought of how gentle he was as he guided her through the beginning of their marriage. She wanted to give him this gift. She could economize until her next deposit of funds. She ought not to be treating herself too often anyway.

She glanced at Mattigan again. "I'll take it. Wrap it up, will you?"

Mattigan nodded with a smile and did so, making a pretty package with a bright ribbon for her. She said her farewells and then she and Hester were off again, back toward the London estate.

And the husband that caused such troubling mixed emotions and desires in her body, mind and soul.

CHAPTER 16

If there was one thing Clarissa had learned to do over the years, it was read the moods of those around her. That night as they stood together in the parlor waiting for the arrival of her parents, Clarissa felt frustration in Roderick. She didn't know the cause, of course, but she still felt tense as she watched him pace the room, seemingly distracted.

"Did your meeting with Mr. Brightly go well?" she asked.

He jerked his head up from where he was staring into his drink and nodded. "Er, yes. He's a good man for the job, I can depend on him. I trust his suggestions for estate improvements."

"Will he join us again before he returns to Kirkwood?"

"Yes. He's in Town for his daughter's wedding, so he'll be busy with that for a while. But I'm certain he'll come again afterward."

"Good. When you know the date, share it with me and I'll set aside time so that I may talk to him about the baskets for tenants we discussed earlier."

"I brought it up to him this afternoon," Roderick said. "So he's thinking about it, as well as making a list for you of people on the estate who may need extra help."

She stared at him a moment. "That was kind of you, to bring up the subject."

"It was important to you," he said, and his dark eyes found hers, holding there, pinning her in place.

She shifted, uncertain of the blooming tingles that had begun in her chest. Desire, yes, but it felt like more.

"Roderick," she began, but before she could finish, Stevenson stepped into the parlor.

"Mr. and Mrs. Lockhart, my lord, my lady."

Her parents burst into the room in what felt like a chaotic explosion. Her mother was wearing feathers and they were shedding lightly behind her, marking a trail that would guarantee she was never lost. Her father, meanwhile, immediately started looking around the room, no doubt tallying up the value of every item in sight.

"Mama, Father," Clarissa managed, sneaking a side glance at Roderick even as she moved forward to greet her parents. His lips were pursed a little, in annoyance, she recognized. Her fault, she supposed, for their marriage had forced him to be linked to her family. And though she tried hard to stick to the rules of Society which said she must obey and honor her parents, it was difficult when they behaved badly.

"...*such* a glorious estate," her mother was saying. "I meant to say it to you at the wedding, but we were all so busy that day. Honestly, I don't think I've ever seen a prettier one."

"Or more richly appointed," her father said with a smile for Roderick. "Hardly needed our Clarissa's little dowry at all, did you?"

Clarissa set her teeth as heat rushed to her cheeks. "Father, we mustn't speak of such crude topics."

"Oh, hush," he grunted at her without looking. "The earl is family now. Family may rib each other a little."

It wasn't ribbing, though. Clarissa knew it. She could see Roderick did, too. And it was all made worse by the fact that the whatever sacrifices her father had made for that *little dowry* he referenced would swiftly be erased by less than a year of her pin money deposits back into their accounts. Of course, Roderick didn't know that. She had written to their solicitor and asked for the account to be managed that way the moment her new husband had told her that she might arrange the funds however she liked.

He'd offered her freedom. And she had been forced to give it away. For a moment she resented it before she pushed those harsh emotions aside. A lady was meant to be moderate in all feelings.

She hated those words so much lately. Even if she continued to do her best to follow them.

"Clarissa?" Roderick stepped to her side and gently set a hand on her lower back. The warmth of his fingers brought her back to the moment and she glanced up at him. He appeared concerned now, not annoyed. At least that was somewhat better.

"I'm fine," she assured him. "I'm sorry, I was just woolgathering."

"Not very polite of you," her father grunted. "Come, why don't we have a drink before supper?"

Roderick straightened a little, his lips tightening, and then he moved toward the sideboard. He was just fiddling with bottles to find the right selection when Stevenson returned to the room.

"I beg your pardon, my lord, but Mr. Brightly sent word about that…" He glanced at Clarissa briefly. "That matter you requested he take care of. You wished to see the note if he sent it so you might immediately reply."

"Yes," Roderick said. "My apologies. This will only take a moment." He nodded to her parents and Clarissa and hustled away.

She sighed at the idea that she would be alone with them, but went to the liquor bottle Roderick had pulled out. "I'll serve you, Father."

"With that?" he blustered. "Come, you know he has better-quality stuff than that."

She pursed her lips and bent to the cabinet. She dug around and found the best scotch she could. When she lifted the bottle, she said, "Will this appease your taste?"

"Very nice." Her father waved her to pour. "Go on then."

She poured one for him and then a sherry for herself and her mother. As she handed out the drinks, she saw them exchange a glance. Her mother elbowed her father lightly and he sipped his drink before he said, "I saw that money was put on our books today. I assume from your pin funds?"

She nodded. "Yes, I would imagine so. I arranged it with Roderick's man. It will be moved to your account after the first of each month."

"Seems it could be more," her mother said.

She wrinkled her brow. "It is a generous sum, Mama. And one I fully control. I couldn't ask for more."

"You could," her father insisted. "Or give us a larger portion of what you are given."

She frowned. As demanded, she had given them two-thirds of her monthly allowance, which meant that after her purchases today, she had nothing left. How was one meant to obtain blood from a stone? Or did they expect her to have no pleasures of her own so they could maintain their lifestyle?

"I—" she began, but before she could finish, Roderick returned to the room. Once more, his mood had changed. His lips were pinched now, his gaze stormy even as he crossed to her and put a hand on her lower back once more.

"Stevenson tells me our supper is ready," he said with a quick glare at her parents. "Why don't we move to the dining room?"

He took her arm to lead the way and she looked up at him. "Is—is something wrong?" she asked softly.

He looked at her then, but just as quickly looked away. "I'm well, I assure you. We can discuss it more later, when we have privacy."

She swallowed hard. What did that mean? What did they have to discuss? But there was no way to press him now. They entered the dining room and took their places at the table.

The night went as well as one could expect. Roderick erased whatever reaction he had from his countenance, certainly her parents didn't recognize anything was wrong. Only every once in a while did Clarissa notice him watching her, his lips thin as if with displeasure.

She had done something wrong and the panic that rose in her was almost overwhelming. Why, she couldn't say. They didn't have a love match, after all. She had no doubt that even if he decided he didn't like her anymore that he would take care of her. He was too gentlemanly to do anything different.

But the idea that he would draw himself away from her felt harder than it should, regardless of any safety he continued to provide. She liked being near him, it turned out. Too much, perhaps. Enough that she was endangering herself with silly emotions.

Supper ended at last and her parents insisted on playing a game of cards after. Clarissa could barely manage herself as she sat across from Roderick and felt the wall between them while she poorly played cards and caused them to lose to her crowing parents.

Eventually, though, her parents moved to the door and they said their goodbyes. Her father leaned in as he said farewell and whispered, "If you care about your parents, after all we did for you, you will find a way to give more."

She drew in a long breath and nodded slowly before she kissed her mother's cheek and she and Roderick stepped out to wave their carriage away into the night. When they were gone, it was like a weight was lifted from her chest. So odd, since she had never realized she felt that way around them until she was in her own home, with a man who seemed to value her autonomy as much as her opinions or company.

"Would you like to come to the parlor for a drink or go to our chamber?" Roderick asked, his tone still rather tight. So it wasn't just her parents who had caused the shift.

She faced him. "I find myself tired. Perhaps our chamber is best."

At least they would have privacy there if he decided to declare their marriage one in name only until he wished to produce an heir with her. To her surprise, he held out a hand. She stared at the long, lean fingers that had brought her so much pleasure over the last week and finally took it.

They were silent as they went up the stairs together, down the long hallway, into their chamber. He didn't stop at the antechamber, but took her into his room, as usual. She worried her lip as the tension between them increased with every move. When he shut the door, he leaned against it and watched her. She fought not to respond, just to wait. Let him make the first move. Not ask for too much when she wanted to beg for just that.

Finally, he drew in a long breath and said, "Tell me what your parents have compelled you to do with your pin money."

Clarissa's mouth fell open at the order and for a moment all her limbs went numb. She shifted. "I-I don't know what you mean."

He shoved off the door and took a long step toward her. "Clarissa." His dark green eyes held her, unwavering, unrelenting. "Tell me. Now."

When Roderick had left Clarissa with her parents before supper to read Brightly's note, he had been nervous, but excited. He was arranging for some changes to the countess chamber at Stratford Manor. A way to surprise her and start to inject some of her personality into their home. When he'd returned, though, when he'd overheard her father demanding she share more of her pin money with him, when he'd realized she'd already turned over a good sum of it to her parents, his good mood had changed.

What he'd wanted to do in that moment was burst into the room, have it out with her greedy parents, come to her defense and burn the world down if need be. It had taken all his control not to do so, to wait so that he could have a private conversation with her, rather than involve her awful parents. This was between them, after all.

Now she was shifting from one foot to the other, wringing her hands before her, unable to meet his gaze. He saw her anxiety in every twitch of her cheek, her upset in the tremble of her hands.

"I-I—" she stammered, her voice wavering.

He took another step toward her and softened his tone and expression. "Please, Clarissa."

She lifted her eyes to his at the *please*. She almost seemed shocked by his gentleness. Which meant she deserved it all the more. But when he reached for her, she pivoted and paced away, around the bed so that it became a barrier between them. She fiddled with items on her bedside table, touched the book under the candle there.

"It's my money, isn't it?" she asked.

He supposed she meant that question to be tart, and it was on some level. It reminded him of how they had begun weeks and weeks ago on her parents' estate. When they had been enemies, rivals. But unlike then, he knew her now. He could see the pain in her eyes, hear the embarrassment in her tone. Her armor could be pierced now. He wanted to make it so she never had to wear it again.

"Yes," he said softly. "The money is yours to do with as you wish."

"Then why interrogate me?" she asked, and threw up her hands. "You obviously overheard something that wasn't meant for your ears."

He started around the bed then, but not fully. He didn't push into her space, just closed a little of the distance. "My duty as your husband is to protect you. To ensure your health and happiness. To be certain you aren't being harmed or taken advantage of."

She shook her head. "They cannot take advantage—they're my parents."

"Oh, they very much can and I would argue they do. And all the more shame on them for it."

All the color left her cheeks at that admonishment. She gripped her hands at her sides. "The duty of a child is to honor their parents' wishes. If they ask for something—"

"Even if it's a cruel request?" he interrupted. "Your pin money is for *your* needs and pleasures. It's given so that you aren't beholden to me for every farthing. Especially given the circumstances of our union, it matters all the more that you can feel some control over your purchases and experiences."

"But they..." She trailed off and shook her head. "They need it."

He barely stopped himself from snorting his derision. It wouldn't help now, not when she was so stuck in this idea that she was responsible for the welfare of people who never bothered to consider hers. "*You* need it. It grants you autonomy. If they wish to steal that from you, they don't have your best interest at heart."

To his surprise, she didn't argue with him. She lifted her gaze to his and held there and for a moment he could read her thoughts. She was considering how her parents had forced this union, with no thought of anything but their own desires.

"Perhaps they never have," she whispered, so softly that he had to strain to hear the words. But there they were. The censure they deserved at last. But she bent her head and let out a little sob. "My apologies for my outburst."

He came the rest of the way around the bed. "*That* wasn't an outburst! I wish you were angry enough to have an outburst. At me, at them, anything!"

Her jaw set. "You are so driven to break me from good behavior, for what? Your own amusement? Because you dislike the concept of propriety so much?"

"That's what this is about?" he asked. "*Propriety*? Who says that being harmed and then forced to take it with that beautiful smile is proper?"

She swept the unlit candle aside and held up the book beneath it, shaking it at him. "This! And *every other* manual on what a lady should be! Every person of authority who ever scolded me for being too much said the same. It is what is expected, the way of our world, whether you want to drag me from it or not."

She tossed the book onto the bed and it bounced toward him.

"And what do the books and authority figures tell you about being human, Clarissa?" He finally gave in to what he'd wanted to do all night and took both her hands.

She stared at their intertwined fingers and then slowly lifted her gaze to his face. There were tears in her eyes, but she blinked them away, not letting him see too far in. A loss he felt down to his soul.

"How very easy for you to say when you've never had to face the world with a smile when all you wanted to do was scream."

He blinked because in that moment he saw it all. Everything she feared and suppressed, everything that secretly weighed her down and made her doubt herself. He saw her vulnerability and all he wanted to do was sooth her, help her, see her true self. He wanted to make himself trustworthy enough that she could give him that true self.

She slipped her hands away and moved around him. She didn't face him, but stood with her back turned, her hands shaking at her sides. "Do you demand I stop giving them the money?"

He let out a long sigh, because as much as he wished to be a safe place for her to fall in that moment, he knew he wasn't. Arguing with her would only put up further walls between them. "It's yours. If you insist, I won't stop you."

"Good." At last she turned toward him. "As I said before we came up, I feel tired. If it's all the same to you, I think I'll sleep in my own chamber tonight."

A pain like being stabbed in the heart ripped through him, stronger than it should be, so sudden that he rested a hand on the edge of the mattress to keep himself from buckling. Since their marriage, she hadn't slept anywhere but beside him.

He cleared his throat. "Very well, Clarissa. Of course."

She swallowed hard and her gaze flitted away from his. "Good night, Roderick."

She was gone then, slipped from his chamber in a few steps, his door closing gently behind her. He stood staring at that door for a moment, longing and sadness filling him, along with confusion. This was a forced union, one they had come to accept. Yes, he wanted her, far more than he had ever believed he could, but they'd agreed it wasn't more. And yet the idea of being without her was painful. The idea of her being alone and hurt burned even more.

He turned away from the door and rested his hands on the edge of her side of the bed. A few inches away from his hands was the book she had waved at him and tossed aside.

The Mirror of Graces.

It looked such a harmless little tome, and yet it seemed to rule Clarissa's every move, every thought. It and books like it had become part of the fabric of her being, a way for her to justify any pain her parents caused, to punish herself for experiencing emotions or desires.

He picked it up and slowly opened the cover, reading over the contents page carefully. He glanced at the door again. If he wanted to be of help to his wife, perhaps what he needed to do was better understand her. So he crossed to the fireplace, took a seat and began to read the book in earnest, hoping it could unlock some of the secrets Clarissa held inside. Ones he shouldn't care about digging deep to excavate, and yet he couldn't help himself.

CHAPTER 17

Wednesday wasn't Roderick's usual day to go to Ripley's Boxing Club, but he found himself there the moment the doors opened regardless. After a night of reading *The Mirror of Graces*, he needed to exert a little rage.

In the ring, he shuffled left, watching the Earl of Ramsbury match his movement. It was only practice and Ramsbury held a pad for training punches. He darted out a hand and slammed it into the center of the pad as hard as he could, sending a ricochet back up through his arm. He shook out his hand as Ramsbury staggered back a fraction.

"Jesus," the earl said as he righted himself. "You're hitting hard today. Problems you wish to discuss?"

Roderick held back a bitter bark of laughter. That was one way to put it. He had a great deal of problems with a book that told women, told *his wife*, that she must hold back all she was. That any reaction was an overreaction, that if she wasn't always thinking about consequences for all actions, from the gown she wore to the words she spoke, they could rain down on her like fire from the sky and tear her world apart. And most of the advice was contrary, making it almost impossible to follow.

"Kirkwood?"

He blinked as he realized he had been staring at Ramsbury for far too long. He swung again, this time with more metered strength. "Your wife," he said slowly. "She was a wallflower, wasn't she?"

A little smile tilted Ramsbury's lips. "Indeed, she was."

Roderick threw a punch again but found no solace in the thunk of flesh against leather. "Was she obsessed with propriety?"

Ramsbury's brows lifted. "I suppose all ladies are in some ways. They're directed to be since childhood."

When Roderick thought of Clarissa's childhood, he swung hard again and nearly deposited himself on his arse in the process. "It's fucking awful."

Ramsbury stepped back and lowered the pads. "What is wrong with you, Kirkwood? You look like you haven't slept and you want to burn the world down. Come, let's sit so you don't hurt yourself or me and talk about it."

Ramsbury motioned toward some of the seats that were faced toward the big ring in the middle of the room. During exhibitions that was where the matches were held. Right now, though, the owner of the club, Campbell Ripley, was locked in battle with one of the professional fighters he trained.

Roderick sighed as he followed Ramsbury to a seat. For a while, they just watched the two men. The fighter was an up-and-comer who went by Lucky, but at the moment he wasn't particularly. Ripley was far faster than his prodigy, his hips swiveling easily, his punches coming out and landing with frustrating accuracy. The boy was doing his best to keep up, though, shifting his weight, ducking under strikes.

Ramsbury let out a laugh. "I think this is why Ripley doesn't let many gentlemen in this time of the morning. It's too obvious we're all amateurs compared to them."

Roderick nodded. That much was very evident. As was his poor behavior a moment ago. He glanced at Ramsbury. "I apologize for my lack of control in the ring. You needn't trouble yourself about my worries."

"I think we're friends of a sort. Certainly, we'll become better ones as I hear my wife and our sister-in-law are determined to become close to your Clarissa. She is all Marianne and Esme could talk about after your wedding."

Roderick couldn't help but smile. "I hope they will be friends. Both of them seem like excellent women and Clarissa deserves to be appreciated by all who meet her."

"Yes," Ramsbury said slowly. "At any rate, I'm happy to discuss whatever you need."

Roderick ran a hand through his hair restlessly. "I would appreciate it. After all, I might normally discuss the problem with Lockhart, but with Clarissa being his cousin and him being firmly unmarried—"

"Yes, I see the problem." Ramsbury nodded.

Roderick dropped his head back, staring up at the ceiling for a moment. "Have you ever encountered one of those comportment books that ladies are sometimes given? One in particular, *Mirror of Graces?*"

Ramsbury's blank expression answered the question even before he shook his head. "No."

"Well, it's a conduct manual. My wife has apparently been so browbeaten her entire life that she believes she must live by its every rule. So I read it last night, every awful word of it, trying to understand."

"That sounds dire."

"It was." Roderick ran a hand through his hair. "I had no idea these were the concepts the women in our lives are drowned in. To be told one must be demure in all things, and yet still be lively? To never allow for any strong emotions, no matter the circumstances?"

Ramsbury pulled a face. "Dear God."

"It says that a woman must never copy another in their behavior."

"Why?" Ramsbury asked slowly.

"For fear of being called a poor reproduction. And yet Clarissa is also expected to follow the same rules as that other woman or risk shunning or worse. It's not possible to do it all."

"It sounds as if there is no allowance for humanity," Ramsbury said.

"Exactly!" Roderick felt the anger rising in him again. "There is no ability for her to stand up for herself. No wonder Clarissa started off in a battle with me. She has been in a battle with herself for all her life. It's all she knows and I am left to watch it tear her apart."

Ramsbury was quiet a moment, simply observing Roderick. "It sounds as though you care a great deal about the pain that causes her."

"I-I do." Roderick blinked. Why did those words feel like a form of confession?

"Have you ever questioned why?"

He shifted in his seat and watched Ripley dodge a punch in the ring before them. It truly felt like he was doing the same, even though this was a friendly conversation he had requested that they have. "It's my duty as her husband to take care of her, is it not?"

"Certainly." Ramsbury shrugged. "At the minimum, it is. What do you want to do?"

Roderick though of Clarissa's face the night before when he'd confronted her about her parents' greedy behavior. She'd looked so defeated beneath the stony exterior she tried to put on to protect herself. It was heartbreaking.

"I want...I want to help her challenge these notions. We may have been forced into this union, but my God, there is no reason for her not to be able to wield the power and influence her new title gives her. I want to help her see that she can still be the epitome of a lady without giving away all her emotions and ignoring her every need."

"And how will you start doing that?" Ramsbury had a little smile on his face, almost smug, which Roderick didn't fully understand. He chose to ignore it and pondered the question. How would one start introducing the power of choice to a person who had given up on her ability to have any?

"The dresses," he said softly.

"I beg your pardon?" Ramsbury said, his brow wrinkling in confusion.

Roderick shook his head. "Nothing, nothing. But you'll need to excuse me. I have something I need to do."

He stood and so did Ramsbury. "I won't keep you, but Kirkwood?"

Roderick had started to go, but he stopped and turned back. "Yes?"

"I told you before that Marianne and I were friends for years before I finally woke up and realized what a treasure she was. Until I saw I was in love with her." Ramsbury took a step toward him. "I know you've always believed in the lightning that sometimes strikes when a man meets the love of his life. But lightning doesn't have to strike out of nowhere. It can strike in the middle of a storm, too. It can strike after the storm has been building on the horizon for weeks, months, even years. If you are planning to challenge Clarissa's beliefs, perhaps you need to challenge some of your own, as well."

Roderick's heart began to pound at those words, his chest aching at the idea. Why was it so terrifying? He swallowed hard. "Perhaps."

"Let me know if I can help."

"I will." Roderick extended a hand and the men shook. "Thank you, Ramsbury."

He pivoted then and hurried from the club. He had a duty to perform, but also a great deal to think about. He only hoped he could sort it all out in his tangled mind.

Clarissa paced her chamber, too restless to work on the letter she'd been trying to write for the last hour. All she could think about was that Roderick had been gone all day. She hadn't seen him since the previous night and their argument in his chamber.

Why had she let that happen? Why had she allowed her emotions to smash on the rocks like some petulant child with no control? Now all that was left was discomfort and problems in their wake.

She needed to repair it. No, that wasn't right. It wasn't just a need. She *wanted* to repair the damage. To go back to the closeness she'd felt with him since their wedding.

She stopped pacing and covered her eyes a moment. "Little fool," she whispered. "This isn't a marriage like that. Even if it seems confusing when you touch or laugh together."

She just had to keep reminding herself of that.

She opened her eyes and her gaze found the wrapped paper package on her dressing table that contained the copy of *Othello* she'd purchased for Roderick the day before. She'd meant to give it to him after supper the previous night, but their argument had stopped her. Perhaps this could be her olive branch?

There was a knock at her door and she turned to find her maid, Hester, at the entrance from the antechamber. "Yes?"

"I'm sorry to disturb you, my lady, but you wished to know when Lord Kirkwood returned from his outing. He's just back now and went straight to his chamber."

Clarissa caught her breath. He was so close and yet he hadn't knocked on her door.

"Th-thank you," she gasped out. "I'll ring when I wish to ready myself for supper."

Hester bobbed out a curtsey and left her. When she heard the outer chamber door close, Clarissa stepped to her mirror and looked at herself. She hadn't slept well and there were light shadows beneath her eyes and her cheeks were pale. She pinched them to bring in some color, smoothed her gown and then took the package before she headed through the antechamber and stood before Roderick's door. It was cracked a little and inside she could hear the splash of water from the basin inside. Her heart was throbbing then, almost like it would burst from her chest, and she placed a hand against the carved wood in the hopes she could ground herself.

It didn't work and so she sighed as she pushed the door fully open and stepped inside. He was standing at the basin, splashing water on his face. His back was to her and he hadn't heard her, it seemed, so she took a moment to stare. He wasn't wearing a shirt and his back flexed in the most distracting way. She wanted to trace the muscles there with her fingertip, her tongue. She wanted to feel him turn into her and his arms come around her like the prior night hadn't even happened.

"Roderick?" she said softly.

He started and turned. Now her breath was gone entirely. His hair was messy, rivulets of water streaked down his handsome face and neck, dripping onto his chest. Her hands shook from wanting to touch him, like a wanton who couldn't control herself. In that moment, she didn't give a damn. She could only hope she hadn't ruined all this, that he might still want her if she could only find the right words to coax him back to her side for a little while.

"Clarissa," he said, and he smiled. The relief that filled her at that gentle expression was almost overwhelming. Tears stung her eyes and she blinked at them so he wouldn't see.

She gathered the paper-wrapped book closer to her chest like it was a shield against the vulnerability she felt in that moment. "I-I didn't know when you would return after…after our quarrel last night."

His expression softened a little. "I worried you."

She didn't want to, but she found herself nodding. He said nothing, but closed the distance between them in a long step. Gently, he removed the book from her arms and set it aside on the closest table, then took her hand. His fingers intertwined with hers, skin stroking skin before he lifted her hand to his lips and gently kissed her knuckles.

"I'm so sorry. I only planned to be gone a short time this morning, but I was distracted by other duties that came up. I should have sent word. If it happens again, I will."

She blinked at the unexpected reaction. "I-I'm being silly."

He shook his head. "Oh, Clarissa. It's not silly to feel as you feel. You can always do that with me."

Something inside of her fluttered and she tugged her hand from his. He let her go and said nothing as she turned toward the table where he had placed her gift. "I'm glad you returned," she said, trying to keep her tone as normal as possible when it felt like her heart was in her throat. "I have something for you."

He looked at the package. "For me?"

She nodded as she picked it up and held it out. "I meant to give it you yesterday until..."

He took it. "A gift?"

He sounded astonished at the idea and now her nerves returned. What it he didn't like it? Or thought it silly? Or didn't even recall the tenuous connection they'd made over Shakespeare weeks ago? She reached for the package. "Perhaps we should wait."

He was already tugging the ribbon. "No, I'd love to see it." The paper fell away and he stared at the book for a moment, his reaction unclear until he looked at her again and she saw his gaze lit up with pure pleasure.

In that moment she knew, in a way she'd tried to ignore and pretend away and keep at a distance, that she was going to end up with her heart broken by him. There was nothing she could do about it.

CHAPTER 18

Roderick couldn't stop staring at the beautiful volume of *Othello* that he held in his trembling hands. This gift Clarissa had chosen and likely paid for with whatever she had left from her pin money after she'd given the rest away to her parents. It was meaningful, personal, something that called back to the first fragile link they'd made to each other back at the country estate.

He looked up at her and when their eyes locked there was lightning. Terrifying, scalding, changing lightning. The kind he had sought all his life and told himself he would find with only one woman.

It was this woman. He didn't only like her or want her or need to protect her.

He *loved* her. And he could see in that same flash of revealing fire that he would only grow to love her more and more deeply as they came to know each other better over the long years of marriage.

She shifted and dropped her gaze away. "You—you're pale."

He shook his head. This wasn't the time to confess this feeling. She wasn't ready, she still had too many defenses up around her. "I don't think anyone has ever given me a gift so precious since I lost my dear parents."

"You like it?" she said, and her relief was palpable.

"I do." He looked at the volume again. "Oh, it's lovely. Perfect."

She smiled and that expression lit up everything in the room, in the world. He set the book down to be fully explored later and reached for her. He was relieved she didn't step away, but allowed him to take her hand and draw her close.

"I love it," he whispered, but he didn't mean the book. It didn't matter that she didn't know that yet. He could still say it as he looked into her eyes.

She lifted her lips and he met them. This was the only place she ever fully let go, when they went to bed together. For now that would be enough and he surrendered to the pleasure of her touch and the connection they would make when they made love.

He drew his fingers into her thick, dark hair, drawing satiny locks down around them as she let out a little sigh of pleasure into his mouth. He took the entry that granted him and deepened the kiss. She tasted of tea and sugar and he loved that flavor of her. Wanted to bathe in it, drown in it. Her arms came up around his neck and she leaned against him, tilting her head to give herself to him.

She was his. More to the point, he was hers. He wanted to show her that. Show her that her ardor and her feelings and her passions would never be too much for him. That she could show them without worry.

He molded her against him, groaning at the pleasure of her body pressed to his. She dug her fingers against his bare back, lifting to him, trembling as her breath became short. His was, too. He stepped back, taking her in. His wet chest had made her white gown stick to her and become more transparent. He smiled at that.

"The one time your wearing white is an entire pleasure," he said with a wicked wink.

She glanced down and saw what he meant. She laughed even as she lifted her hands to cover herself.

"Oh no," he murmured, and grabbed her hand, lowering it and pulling her to the basin where there was still water. "I like it."

He dipped a hand into the water and then pressed it to her breast, rubbing a thumb against her nipple. She arched a little, a shaky exhalation of breath letting him know he was pleasing her.

He wetted his hand again and dragged it down the apex of her body, making her dress stick to her stomach. She wore a chemise beneath, of course, but it still let him see the shape of her. The wonderful curves of her.

She gazed up at him, lower lip trembling. She caught his hand, and for a moment he thought she might push it away, demand they stop this because it wasn't proper. But to his happy surprise, she instead moved his hand lower, across her hip and then to her thighs. He could see the soft pink flesh of them where her dress was dampened and he licked his lips in anticipation.

"I think I ought to dunk you in water every afternoon," he murmured. "Make you my mermaid. See how wet you can be."

She arched a brow. "I have a feeling you're not talking about my clothing. Or…or are you?"

He laughed. "You're learning so quickly, my lady. I want you wet between your thighs, I want you aching for me. Ready for me to take you and remind you that you are mine." Her pupils dilated and he smiled. That grip on what she deemed proper was so much lighter here in his arms. "Tell me you're mine," he said.

"I'm yours," she whispered after the slightest hesitation. "I'm yours. Make me yours."

He couldn't play with her anymore. Not when his emotions felt so powerful, not when she was staring up at him with her eyes glistening with desire.

He found her mouth again, this time with more passion and drive, and let his hand slide down her side. He cupped her bottom and she moaned into his mouth. He gripped the back of her thigh and lifted her leg, wrapping her around him so that when he ground against her he hit that sweet cleft of her sex even through her damp clothes.

"Please," she whimpered, staggering backward as he moved her to the bed. "Please."

He nodded as he continued to kiss her. They fell against the bed together, him covering her body. Her leg locked around his thigh tighter and she lifted with a shivering sigh. His cock was throbbing, echoing all his love for her, demanding he pour it over her and into her. At least in this they could be one.

He found the buttons along the front of her bodice and tugged them free with one hand while he kept kissing her. When the gown parted, he shoved it aside, along with her damp chemise beneath. One perfect breast popped free and he latched his lips around the pebbled nipple, sucking as she writhed beneath him and rubbed herself against him in the same rhythm they would eventually use when he took her.

He pushed the entire dress down to her waist and sucked the opposite nipple. She drew her hands into his hair, holding him there, then pushing him down. He lifted his eyes to her, smiling against her skin.

"You want my mouth on you?" he asked.

Her cheeks filled with pink and she turned her head away. He sucked her nipple harder and she gasped and glared at him.

"I want to hear what you want," he said. "Tell me you want my tongue on you. You want to wrap your thighs around my shoulders and rock against me until you are shattered. Tell me."

"I want that," she gasped out. "I want you to...to...to lick me. Please, please."

He could see how difficult it was for her to ask for what she wanted and so it was good enough. A little step forward, one he would cling to.

He drew his mouth down, tugging her dress as he did, hearing some of the fabric rend as he shoved it away with his bare foot. He expected her to protest, but she only moaned louder as he settled himself between her legs and began to draw the words "I love you" against the wet, trembling flesh of the wife he adored.

~

I f she had been asked before her marriage, Clarissa wouldn't have ranked heated ardor as one of her highest desires in a husband. She wouldn't have even understood what it meant. But having Roderick perched between her legs, his big hands pressed into her thighs to spread them wide, his tongue working in a rhythm against her tingling clitoris, the ardor was everything. *He* was everything.

She pushed that thought aside and focused instead on the mounting sensations created by his expert tongue. She lifted into him, rising with the intensity of the waves of pleasure building deep within her. She reached for it, knowing it well by now, needing it and the release it would give. Release he gave from all her troubles and thoughts and worries. When it hit, she gripped the coverlet with both hands, legs shaking and gripping around his broad shoulders. He didn't let up, continuing to suck and lick in the same endless rhythm until her cries faded and her tremors subsided.

Then he leaned forward, caging her in with his body, his mouth finding hers and letting her taste the slick, wicked proof of her loss of all control. She reveled in it, this brief respite from responsibility. She wanted more, she was greedy for it, and so she lifted against him, feeling the proof of his desire hard and thick against her thigh through his trousers.

He chuckled against her mouth and then straightened, shedding the rest of his clothing swiftly before he settled back against her. He was watching her now as he aligned his cock to her, studying her as he took her in a long, smooth stroke.

She cried out again as he moved through her, but when she tried to turn away from the intensity of his stare, he cupped her chin and held her there gently, forcing the eye contact. Forcing her to hold on him as he took her slowly, gently, almost tortuously. The pleasure was easy to find the second time. It lingered from his mouth and was stoked by the grind of his pelvis to hers. But he denied it, keeping her on the edge instead of letting her fall over as she wished to do. She lifted harder, trying to demand, and he smiled.

"That's right," he whispered.

He caught her hips and rolled on the bed, shocking her by moving her over him. They were still connected, his cock still buried deep, and she couldn't help but arch her hips against him. Her eyes widened. This position felt different. She controlled where his cock hit her, how she found her pleasure and gave his.

He was still holding her gaze and he nodded. "Take it," he urged. "Let go and use me."

She shivered at those two words. *Use me.* What a concept that she could control him, make him dance on her string, take only what she desired without thought of consequences. She rested her hands on his shoulders and rose up a fraction, changing the angle of their joined bodies once more.

"Such a good girl," he growled.

Her body rolled with pleasure and she barked out a little cry from it. She did it again, again, taking him, increasing the pace, thinking of nothing but the building pressure between her legs. He lifted to meet her, his pupils almost black they were dilated so far from desire.

She came, crushing her mouth to his as her hips thrust out of control and he dug his fingers into them, marking her with his power even as he gave her her own. He groaned against her lips, coming deep within her, the heat of him only stoking the flames of release.

But at last she collapsed on his chest, panting with the exertion of pleasure. It had been different this time. Something had shifted between them, but she couldn't name it. All she knew was that when his arms came around her she felt...safe. That was a fallacy, but she sank into it regardless, smiling when he gently kissed her temple, her cheek.

His fingers traced patterns along her back and she shivered at that touch. The things this man could do to her. Make her forget. Make her want.

She shifted and he let her go as she rolled onto her back and stared up at the ceiling. The kissing couples painted in relief there were taunting her. None of them looked troubled by thoughts.

"I don't think we should go downstairs," he said, rolling on his side.

His hand settled on her hip, gentle, warm weight that once again drew all those thoughts away far too easily.

"No?" she asked, forcing herself to look at him. God, he looked so handsome mussed from all those sinful things he did to her. How could he look so perfect when he was imperfect while she felt nothing but pressure when she did the same?

"No. I want to stay here all afternoon. All night."

"In this bed?" she said with a laugh.

He nodded and wasn't laughing. He wasn't teasing. He meant it. "I want to stay in this bed with you, Clarissa, and test how many ways I can make you moan my name."

"Oh," she said softly, her body already tingling at the thought. "And what about supper?"

"I already had mine," he said with a wicked wink.

Her laugh increased at his cheek and she swatted him lightly with her palm. "You cad."

"When we're hungry, I'll call for something to be brought up. We'll feed each other and drink a little too much wine and then I'll lay you down on the rug in front of the fire and make you forget your name as you beg me for release."

She stared at him. The heaven of what he suggested was so tempting, even though she knew that the surrender he was talking about violating at least some of the rules of propriety. But in that moment, she didn't give a damn.

"What if I want to make *you* forget your name?" she asked, and heat instantly filled her cheeks at the bold question.

He tugged her against him. "Oh, I have so many things to teach you that will make you do that, my lady. So many things."

She groaned as he kissed her and forget everything else, at least for a little while. She could return to reality soon enough. There was no other choice.

CHAPTER 19

It was four days after her appointment with Miss Swanlea that the seamstress made an appointment for a fitting at Clarissa's home. She'd been led to the countess's chamber upon arrival and set up her things, and now Clarissa stepped into the room to do the fitting for the white gown.

She wasn't as excited about it as she normally felt with a new outfit. But the idea of yet another white gown fell flat now and she forced a smile as she moved toward the seamstress.

"Miss Swanlea," she said, acknowledging when the woman curtseyed slightly. "I am thrilled to see you and cannot wait to enjoy what you've made."

"I hope you'll like both items," Miss Swanlea replied, and then stepped back from the small portable rack where she had carefully hung the gowns and Clarissa's coat.

Clarissa stared. Yes, there was the white gown in the fabric she had requested, but next to it was another dress. This one in the pretty pink fabric she had examined at the showroom and rejected despite her feelings about it.

"What is that?" she asked, unable to look away. The dress was gorgeous, with a slightly lower neckline than she normally wore and exquisite finishing touches like the wide ribbon along the bottom hem of the dress and the velvet band around the high waist.

Miss Swanlea smiled. "A surprise from the earl, my lady. He appeared in my shop the day after your measurement session and requested I make another gown for you. He wanted to know any fabric that particularly caught your eye and then chose from the colors you had liked."

Clarissa moved past her and reached for the gown. Her fingers brushed the soft silk fabric with its fine damask pattern. It was so beautiful, even though it wasn't the white she felt she had to wear for propriety's sake.

But then again, she knew many women—most women, even—who wore color, didn't she? Marianne and Esme, for example, were both women she admired and they wore beautiful gowns that weren't white. Why couldn't she do the same? Why couldn't she embrace her own style, rather than stick to the one her books had insisted she wear so she wasn't putting fashion over elegance.

No, she couldn't think like that. But nor would she show her upset to Miss Swanlea. It wasn't the seamstress's fault that Roderick had asked for the dress to be created. She would take it up with him later.

"Where should we begin?" she asked with a bright smile.

Miss Swanlea motioned to the low step she had already set and Hester came from the corner of the room. Together they helped Clarissa into the white gown first. They chatted, with Clarissa trying to stay focused as Miss Swanlea made little markings for final adjustments she'd make to the gown.

When that was finished, they moved to the pink dress. Clarissa squeezed her eyes shut as they put her into the silk, and tried not to revel in the softness of the fabric. She knew it was just silk, like so many of her other gowns, but it still felt different, it felt like temptation, itself, to put it on.

At last, though, she was in it and she opened her eyes and looked at the full-length mirror Hester had drawn into the room so she could see the gowns herself. She caught her breath. Even with it not perfectly fitted, she could see it was the finest gown she'd ever owned.

The color was perfect for her skin. It made her cheeks look lightly rouged and her eyes dance, the little flecks of green within the brown standing out in a new way. She felt...*pretty* as she stared at herself and her eyes filled with tears that she blinked away as the same conversations were held about this gown as had been with the first.

When it was finished and Clarissa dressed again in her old gown—white, of course—and it felt so boring as she stared at it, she watched as Hester took her freshly lined coat away. She turned toward Miss Swanlea and smiled. "You do wonderful work, as always."

"Thank you, my lady. And I must say that the pink truly does suit you. If you wish any other gowns with color, I have so many ideas for fabrics that will make you shine just as brightly."

Clarissa's heart lodged in her throat. She'd been going to Miss Swanlea for her clothing for a few years now and she'd never seen the woman so excited to make her something. She inclined her head. "You are too kind. Now I'll excuse myself. Take your time collecting your things. Hester will escort you out when you are ready."

"Good day, my lady."

Clarissa waved and then stared downstairs. She'd been told Roderick was in the library before she'd gone to meet with the seamstress. Normally she wouldn't interrupt him in his reading, but in that moment she had to have a conversation with him. Though what she would say, she wasn't entirely certain.

The rotunda room was where the library was housed and it had always been Roderick's favorite chamber of the home. The bedchamber was becoming his second favorite. But today he sat in his favorite chair beside the fire, reading the bound edition of *Othello* Clarissa had gifted him a few days before. The lithographs included in the volume were exquisite. Sometimes he spent a long time just looking at the details of one before he turned the page to continue reading the play.

The door to the library opened and he lifted his gaze to watch Clarissa come in. Storm in was more like it. Her dark eyes were alive with emotion and her hands were fisted at her sides.

"Clarissa," he said, and set the book aside as he stood to greet her. "How was the fitting?"

"Why did you go to Miss Swanlea behind my back and order a gown?" she asked.

He stared at her a moment. He couldn't tell if she was angry or sad or thrilled by the fact he had done so. She was so very good at hiding, perhaps even from herself.

"I wanted to give you a gift," he said carefully. "Just as you did me. A surprise. The fabric was lovely, Miss Swanlea said you had admired it. I think it must look beautiful on you. I cannot wait to see it."

Her lips tightened. "I can't…a woman may, of course, wear color, but white is always a sign of an elegance of mind, not a dedication to the frivolity of fashion."

He shook his head. "That is from your book, isn't it? I recognize the turn of phrase too well."

"My book?" She shook her head, her eyes wild. "What do you mean?"

"I read *Mirror of the Graces*," he said, and watched as the high color in her cheeks bled away. "The night you slept in your own chamber last week. You left it there and I needed to understand why my delightful wife feels she must turn herself inside out for rules that I cannot even fathom."

"You read it only to dismiss it?" she asked, her hands dropping to her sides. "To dismiss what's important to me?"

"Are you angry that I did?" he asked, and stepped closer. He saw her tense. "Be angry, Clarissa. I beg of you. Tell me to sod off. Tell me I violated your boundaries."

"No," she murmured. "You won't make me forget moderation."

"Moderation is for drinking," he said, throwing up his hands since she wouldn't. "Not for feelings. I have the deepest regard for what is important to you, Clarissa. And respect for how you comport yourself regularly. Not because of some book. I watch you in all your glory with those around you. What makes you a lady is how much attention you bestow when others speak. You make everyone feel as if they're the center of the world when they're near you. I admire your kindness to all, regardless of their rank. I definitely admire your wit, which occasionally cuts me and always makes me laugh."

She lifted her chin and he saw the sparkle of tears in her eyes now. He moved closer again. "*None* of those things came from the bloody book. In fact, the only good advice I found in the wretched pages of that thing was that you ought not wear cosmetics with ingredients that might kill you. Otherwise, the rest is trash that not even a saint could live up to."

She pivoted away with a gasping cry that cut him down to the bone. The pain seemed to radiate from her now, something she could no longer control.

He touched her arm gently, not turning her back, but letting her feel the weight of his support. His love, even if he wouldn't yet name it.

"Why did your lock yourself to this?" he asked gently. "Please, I want to know."

"My pain for your pleasure?" she asked, her voice barely carrying.

He did turn her now, cupping her chin to make her look at him. "Never. Because your hurts are mine. I want to understand you."

One of those tears fell at last, sliding down her cheek as she sucked in a shuddering, pained breath. "If I don't control everything, control myself, bad things will happen."

~

She said the words she'd never spoken to another person out loud. She heard how foolish they sounded and waited for him to laugh at her or dismiss her. But instead he cupped her cheek, his expression softened in understanding and support. It nearly buckled her knees. He made her feel like she could depend on him.

What a dangerous thought that was.

"Bad things happen, no matter what we do," he said gently. "It has nothing to do with your behavior."

She shook her head. "That's not true. I can make things right if I try harder. I can fix things for my parents, for you, for—for—"

His brow wrinkled a little and he took her hand. "You don't have to fix anything for me. You're not responsible for that. And what do you have to fix for your parents? What have you ever done wrong when it came to them?"

She stared at him. She didn't want to give him the answers, it felt so vulnerable to do so. But perhaps if she did, he'd leave her be. If he understood, he'd stop challenging her to be more than she was. He'd understand why she couldn't be and then she could rebuild the shell around herself and focus on what was right. What was proper.

"I was born, that's what I did wrong," she said softly. "And I wasn't what they wanted. I could never be what they wanted. What they needed. My father is a younger son of an earl, and the frivolous one at that. They spent all their money because they always believed they'd be able to raise themselves through their children."

As she began her story, Roderick drew her to the settee. They took a place together and he cupped her hand in both of hers, his eyes focused on her face.

She chose to concentrate on her lap because she didn't want to look at him when she spilled out the emotions she had tried for years to hold in moderation. She feared what it would look like when they were finally free.

"They had me within the first year of their marriage. As a girl I would likely cost them more than I brought them..." She glanced up at him. "That's what they told me, many times."

He flinched but didn't interrupt.

"They continued to try, but never succeeded in having another viable child." She shut her eyes. "They would fight about it, I could hear them at night. But they always pretended it wasn't happening. Put on their smiles in the light of day. As I got older, I began to feel the pressure of their desperation."

"Because they began to realize you were their only hope."

She nodded. "Yes. They altered their plans. Instead of having many sons and daughters, gathering support from them and their good marriages, they would have to manipulate the best marriage they could through me. To do that, they spent even more that they didn't have. Presented a front and educated me in everything I would need to land the husband they saw as appropriate." She shivered. "But it was never enough. *I* was never enough. I could be more, though. I could be better if I just…try harder."

"Clarissa," he said softly.

She shook her head. "I could be. I could make them happy and then they'll…they'll…" She trailed off because what she wanted to say was a stab wound to her heart.

"What will they do?" he asked.

She drew in a few breaths, squeezed her hands into fists so they'd stop shaking. "They'd like me. They'd…they'd love me."

He let the statement hang in the air for a long moment before he touched her face gently. "You are so worthy of love without earning it. You earn it by simply existing."

She sucked in a breath. He made it sound so simple when it never had been for her. Love was transactional. It was a carrot, or a stick when it was withdrawn after a mistake. And he made it sound like something soft and gentle and unwavering. Sort of like what she saw when she saw Ramsbury and Marianne together. Or Esme and Delacourt.

"I don't know," she whispered. "I didn't explain it right."

A sad smile tilted his lips. "You did. You explained it perfectly. That doesn't change that I *hate* that you were taught otherwise by people who should have valued and treasured you. That they let their own failings fall upon you like that."

She shrugged even though saying this meant so much more than that dismissive action implied. "But doesn't it make me better? To strive for perfection is a lofty goal. And they encouraged it by presenting me with books on comportment like the one you read. The rules ground me. They let me know my place."

He stared at her for a long moment and it was like he was seeing her for the first time. "When the world is chaotic and difficult to manage a way through, as it seems it was in your parents' home, I would assume the rules gave you something to lean on. A way to understood what to do, how to respond."

She shivered because what he was saying felt so…right. She never examined her childhood very closely. Her memories were foggy and unpleasant and they made her sad when she pondered them. But chaos was the way to describe her life at home. Her life up until this man had rode up to her doorstep and turned everything upside down. Or was it right side up? When he talked to her like this, offered her peace like this…she felt right side up for the first time in her life.

"But you must see how behaving properly could make someone see me as a good bet for marriage."

"You never aspired to love?" he asked softly, and his hands tightened around hers. "You never thought to wish for someone who would love you for yourself?"

She tilted her head and looked into those dark green eyes. A calm peace like a deep forest she could lose herself in forever. But then how would she get out when he tired of her? Or if he found that woman who made him fall head over heels the moment he met her?

She turned away. "You wouldn't understand. You speak with such love for your parents."

"I suppose that's true," he said carefully, as if considering her statement. "I do view love differently after seeing it through the lens of their relationship to each other and to me. But I was adrift when they died so suddenly. I do understand that feeling of not knowing my place. Of needing to be grounded by something, anything. Though I likely chose worse options than diving into proper behavior."

She smiled a little. "So that's how you obtained your reputation as rake."

"I suppose it is." He smoothed a lock of hair away from her forehead. "I'm so sorry, Clarissa. I mean that from the bottom of my heart. However, the circumstances that created your dedication to rules and propriety are no longer what surround you. I could be…I want to be… your true north. Your stability, the thing you can depend on rather than all those rules that make you question yourself."

She blinked at that idea. He must feel sorry for her to suggest such a thing, because he could mean it no other way. Just a few weeks ago, he'd declared he didn't love her. That he had lost what hope he had for his future when they became engaged. How could she depend on him now, knowing they were destined to be friends and nothing more? Their futures would be intertwined, surely, but not the way he suggested.

Even if it sounded like heaven. Even if she could so easily picture it when she looked into his eyes. That future positively danced before her, teasing her. Taunting her.

Making her want things she couldn't have and that hurt to pretend could ever be real.

"Depending on others? That's too dangerous," she said, and drew her hands from his before she rose to her feet.

There was a moment when he almost looked heartbroken by that statement. That couldn't be true, and it was gone as soon as she'd recognized it.

He nodded slowly and also stood. "I understand why. I'll have to prove that I'm worthy of such a risk." She wrinkled her brow, but didn't have a chance to respond, because he continued, "But please don't shut out how you feel. Who you are. These rules aren't *right*, even if you think them proper. And I lo—care for you too much to watch you be crushed beneath their weight."

She blinked. He'd started to say *love*. Or she thought he had.

Another lie he was telling or she was hearing. Her mind spun, though, and she could scarcely breathe.

"I'll consider it," she managed to whisper. She stepped to the door. "I have a few things to do. I'll see you at supper."

He nodded and didn't try to stop her when she left the room. She closed the door behind her and let out a sob she'd been holding back before she fled to her chamber and locked the door behind her. The idea of moderation in her feelings was becoming harder and harder to achieve. Especially when the man she had linked her life to kept beckoning her closer, threatening her heart and her future with pretty words.

∾

Roderick watched as his valet left the room. With a sigh, he moved to the candle on his dressing table. His evening had been…odd, at best. Clarissa had waited until the last possible moment to join him before supper and the meal had been quiet. He felt her withdrawal, her walls, and all he wanted to do was tear them down.

But he couldn't. They were her protection. He wouldn't strip them away by force. He wanted her to see she didn't need them. But after hearing what she'd gone through, how she had been ground into dust beneath the feet of her family, he understood how difficult that would be.

He only hoped she wouldn't walk away from him permanently to save herself from the grief she feared he'd cause.

As if on cue, his door opened and she stood there in her nightrail. Her hair was down around her shoulders, sleek and dark, and her gaze moved over him. She said nothing, but stepped inside, closed the door behind her and then came across to him at the bed.

He set the candle down and shivered when she wrapped her arms around him. Her mouth lifted and he met it, closing his arms around her and letting her mold to him.

This tiny surrender wasn't what he wanted, not truly. But for now it would be enough. He lowered her onto the bed, writing his I love yous on her skin, feeling her surrender those hated walls if only to his passion.

And hoped that was only the beginning to what they could be to each other.

CHAPTER 20

Another week had gone by and Roderick was restless. His wife was perfect. No one could deny it. She did all her duties with a smile. Her kindness toward the servants only increased and it seemed they all adored their new mistress. When she hosted friends, she always impressed with her easy skill at making all feel welcome and special.

But despite whatever advancement he made in their relationship when he took her to his bed and awakened her passion, she let none of that bleed into their everyday existence. She spoke to him of surface topics, she pulled away from anything she feared and she hadn't yet worn the pink gown he'd had designed for her, even though the completed dress had been delivered a few days before.

Could he live like this? Falling more deeply in love with her every day but never being able to mount the walls she built like a princess in a tower? He wasn't sure. He wasn't ready to give up the idea that one day he would find the weakness to that tower and bring it down.

"My lord?"

He turned away from the window in his study and found Stevenson waiting for him. "Yes, Stevenson?"

"Lady Kirkwood's parents have arrived for tea," Stevenson said.

"You were, of course, meant to be out before your morning meeting was canceled. And I fear Lady Kirkwood is engaged in a household issue and will be a few more moments."

Roderick pursed his lips, wondering why she hadn't told him her parents were coming. Though he supposed it made sense. She knew he was upset at their taking advantage of her financially and even more so by how they had made her feel not enough.

"I'll join them," he said. "Which parlor are they in?"

"The blue parlor, my lord," Stevenson said with a grateful smile. "I'll inform her ladyship that you have joined them."

"Very good."

Roderick tugged his clothing into place as he went down the hallway to the parlor in question. He was about to push the door open when he heard his father-in-law talking.

"—blasted girl had one job to do. We got her married off to a rich earl and you'd think she could manage to be grateful enough to support us."

"Well, tell her so when she comes in," Mrs. Lockhart said. "She owes us."

Roderick's nostrils flared and he pushed the door open. "Good afternoon," he said, his tone clipped.

They both turned toward him and suddenly they were all obsequious welcome, bowing and tittering.

"We did not know we'd have the pleasure, my lord," Mrs. Lockhart said. "Our daughter led us to believe you would be out during our visit."

"A late change of plans," Roderick said as he fought not to glare at the woman. "Clarissa thought I would be out."

"It seems she should have a better handle on her husband's schedule," Mr. Lockhart blustered. "I hope she's doing her duties as countess well enough."

Roderick drew in a long breath to remain calm. "She is perfect."

Her father snorted but said nothing else on the subject. Instead, he crossed to where the tea service was and examined the biscuits and tea. "That girl knows I like the raspberry jam best. Honestly," he muttered. "You would think she could keep one simple thing in her mind."

Roderick moved forward. "I'm not fond of raspberry," he said with a frown. "And we hardly ever have it in the house because of that. And your daughter keeps a great many things in her mind, all of which seem to be about ensuring you two are happy. Even though you clearly think little of her feelings."

Mrs. Lockhart spun on him. "I-I cannot imagine what you mean?"

He drew in a deep breath. He'd told Clarissa she could manage her own affairs and perhaps he should allow her just that. But with these two disparaging her in his house, in *her* house, it was too much to bear.

"I have become aware that she is giving you two-thirds of her monthly pin funds," he said. "Even though those are supposed to be for her pleasure and her good. Why would you do such a thing?"

Both his in-laws' eyes went wide at that question and they exchanged a quick glance. Roderick searched for embarrassment at their base behavior. Regret. He saw none. Only calculation of how they should handle him so that they could continue a lifestyle they could only support on Clarissa's back.

"Our daughter's pleasure has always been to take care of her parents," Mrs. Lockhart said. "We raised her well."

Roderick pursed his lips. "Was that her pleasure because to deny you only brought her harm? She turned out well, but I would argue it was despite the way she was raised, not because of it."

Mr. Lockhart's nostrils flared. He was clearly the kind of man whose inflated sense of entitlement didn't allow him to accept criticism. He would lash out, that was evident even before he said, "Well, she has plenty under you, doesn't she? She can afford to help her parents, who took care of her."

"As was their duty," Roderick said. "And for which she *owes* nothing."

"Marcus," Mrs. Lockhart said, and grabbed her husband's arm.

He shook her off and continued to stare at Roderick. "If she can afford to share her wealth, I see no reason not to tell her my requirements."

Roderick slowly counted to ten to calm his increasing anger. "I want you to see it from her side. The reason for that pin money would give her some independence. The only thing you knew about me when you forced this union was that I was titled and rich. What if I had been an ogre? What if I was the sort of man who hurt or controlled her? What if she needed that allowance for her daily requirements, not just niceties?"

Her mother stared at him like he'd sprouted a second head. It seemed she truly didn't understand the concept. "If Clarissa displeases a husband enough that he lifts a hand against her or punishes her, it sounds as though she needs to apply herself more. It wouldn't be our problem, would it?"

Roderick's mouth dropped open at the idea that they would blame Clarissa if she had been forced by them into a marriage with a man who would harm her. "You two are monsters. To care so much for yourselves and so little for her well-being. It stops now."

Before her parents could answer, Clarissa burst into the room, her face pale and her eyes darting toward him. "Oh, I'm here. Please don't argue. I'm here now."

"And good you are," Mr. Lockhart said, and now his ire turned on Clarissa. "I think you have been complaining to your husband. Turning him against us."

"No." Clarissa shook her head. "I would not do such a thing, I promise you."

Roderick ached at her tone. At how broken and fearful she sounded. "Clarissa, they hold no power over you anymore," he said softly. "They cannot take anything away from you, you don't have to protect them from the consequences of their own poor actions. You deserve better. You always have."

Clarissa jerked her attention to him and their eyes locked. He stepped toward her, all the love he felt for her rising up in him. But at last she bent her head and then returned her gaze to her parents. "Roderick knows I've been sharing my pin money with you. He's kindly concerned about my well-being. Perhaps overly so. I have no intention of changing our agreement. You needn't cause trouble."

Her mother's lips twitched. "Cause trouble? It isn't us. It's you. He might not know better, but you should."

Clarissa's lips parted and she glanced at Roderick again. "Why—why would you think he wouldn't know better? What does that mean?"

"His parents are dead, that's all I meant," her mother said with the same blank expression she seemed to always have when she fired shots toward her daughter.

Roderick moved forward, but to his surprise, Clarissa was already rushing toward her parents. There was no deference to her now, only flared nostril indignation as she said, "How *dare* you bring that up? How dare you throw his greatest loss, his deepest pain, into his face?"

"Oh, please!" her father snorted. "It happened years ago. It's merely an observation."

Clarissa shook her head, disgust on her face. "This man has been nothing but decent, even when you two were anything but. By your behavior, you dishonored not just me, but yourselves, and yet he is still a gentleman."

Her parents exchanged a look, seemingly shocked that she would speak in such a way. "I dare say you ought to have some respect for your elders, Clarissa," her father blustered.

She blinked and then shook her head. "Roderick is worth ten of you, Father. And I know that, even if I continue to politely ignore it in your company. This is *his* home and I am *his* wife. Understand that I shall ever take his side in all things. You'll never turn me against him for your purposes. If you press me on that, you won't like the results."

There was a long moment of silent shock and Roderick's was the largest share of it. Here Clarissa refused to stand up for herself, but when it came to defending him she surrendered all her thoughts on what she owed her family. He had not had a champion like that, someone to fight at his side like some avenging angel, for many years. He'd forgotten how wonderful it was.

"I think perhaps it's time for you two to go," Roderick said softly as he motioned for the door.

"I think so," Mr. Lockhart said, and grabbed his wife's arm. They stormed from the room together, Clarissa's father calling for their carriage and slamming the front door with great force.

Clarissa wobbled a little and braced her hand on the back of a chair. Her breath was rough and harsh as she tried to gather herself. Then she looked up at him. "I'm sorry, Roderick."

He shook his head and crossed to her, taking her hand and lifting it to her chest. What he felt couldn't be contained now. He needed her to know it, to feel it, to begin to trust it, or at least understand that he was going to fight for it.

He needed to take a risk so that she would begin to feel comfortable to do the same.

He drew a deep breath of his own and said, "Clarissa, I love you."

Clarissa already felt wobbly after the confrontation with her parents, but now she nearly toppled over. It was only that Roderick steadied her that kept her on her feet. She stared at him, uncertain now if all of this was just some heated dream.

It had to be. She knew where they stood.

"You don't mean that," she whispered at last.

He shook his head. "I very much do." She tried to pull away, but he didn't release her. "I know it's frightening. It is for me, too. Love can mean loss. I felt it myself and it was terrible. But it's also so beautiful. Our life could be so beautiful, Clarissa, if you let me love you. If you find it in your heart to try to love me in return."

"I thought you believed in lightning. Instant recognition," she said. "We both know that isn't us."

"I do believe in lightning. I am struck down by your mercy. The lightning hit after the storm began, that's all. I never should have been so rigidly dedicated to the idea that it could only come in one way. Life isn't rigid. It's what I've been trying to tell you. You taught me that instead."

She was shaking so hard, she feared letting go of the back of the chair. What could she say to these words, so sweet and yet so confounding? This man loved her? She wanted to burst into tears. To collapse into a puddle. To spin around the room in circles. Joy and terror and disbelief all at once.

"I've overwhelmed you," he said. "I'm sorry. I only realized I couldn't wait to tell you. I needed you to know. You can have all the time in the world to come to terms with this. To think about it. But understand that I intend to woo you most ardently. I intend to prove to you that those two jackals who just stormed out of our home were wrong. Every part of you is lovable. Every bit of you is enough. You are and never could be too much to adore. And I do adore you."

Tears stung her eyes, but she couldn't control them. Moderation was far out of reach and so they fell, dragging down her cheeks, over-whelming her. With a gasp, she pulled away from him. "I need...I need to think. I need...I need to go, to gather myself."

"Yes," he said. "I can have a carriage brought if you need to go somewhere. Please, not to your parents."

"No," she breathed. "To...I don't even know who I could go to." Then she stopped. "Lady Ramsbury. Marianne. She was so kind in the countryside."

He smiled a little. "I think that's a fine idea. Talk to her about it. You deserve to have friends who you can confide in, be yourself with. Let me call the carriage."

He stepped out with a backward look for her. She leaned forward, pressing her forehead against the edge of the chair back where her hands rested. How was this real? How was this happening.

But no, she had to gather herself. She stood and smoothed her gown, trying to put herself back together. Roderick returned. "The carriage is being brought. Let me help you?"

She nodded. This was all so dreamlike. This man had confessed to the deepest, most powerful feelings for her, and now he was helping her run away from him and them. Giving her control, the one thing she'd always reached for and perhaps never really had.

He gave it like it was water or food, something to share for sustenance, not withhold for cruelty.

They stepped out and he waved off a footman waiting to help her into the vehicle. He opened the door, but didn't move to help her up. Instead he cupped her cheeks, lowered his lips to hers, and kissed her.

He had kissed her so many times, but this was different. It was so gentle, so filled with the very love he had just declared. She found herself clinging to his arms, lifting into him like she could escape the spinning terror of her heart with him.

But at last he let her go. "I love you," he whispered, then handed her up into the vehicle, closed the door and waved to her from the front door.

She pulled away from him, but there was no peace in escape. In fact, now that he was not there to ground her anymore, she felt more adrift than ever. And more uncertain as to how to respond to the man who offered her a life she'd never dared dream of.

A life that felt almost too good to be true.

CHAPTER 21

The moment Clarissa was brought to wait for Marianne in her fine parlor, she knew she'd made a mistake. It wasn't proper to show up uninvited, face streaked with tears to a countess's house. Even a friend's house. A lady sent a card, she inquired, she planned. She didn't invade.

And yet Clarissa didn't leave. She needed to see that friend. To talk about this. That somehow carried more weight in that moment than what any guidebook had ever said she should do.

The door opened and she turned. When not just Marianne, but her sister-in-law Esme, the Countess of Delacourt, entered the room, Clarissa blushed.

"Oh, I've intruded," she said. "I shouldn't. I'm being ridiculous and rude and—"

Without a word, Marianne rushed across the room to her and suddenly Clarissa was enveloped by a gentle hug. "Oh, dearest, please. Stop berating yourself. I can see you're terribly upset. I'm so happy you're here and so is Esme."

"Very happy," Esme assured her, and Clarissa looked up and saw the other woman was getting tea.

Marianne guided her to the settee and sat with her. Esme returned with a cup for her and then took her place in a chair across from them.

"What has happened?" Esme asked gently. "Are you well? Is there danger?"

Clarissa blinked. Danger? "Er, no. Not danger. Not the way I think you mean."

Esme relaxed a little and nodded. "Good. Then tell us what has happened. What brought you here without warning and with your eyes so wide and wild?"

"I don't know how to say it," Clarissa burst out. "I don't even know how to feel it. A lady is to have moderation, isn't she? She isn't supposed to have emotions wash over her like some wave that can sweep her away. It's not right."

Marianne grabbed both her hands. "What's not right is tormenting yourself like this. Tell us what happened."

Clarissa drew in a long breath, unable to fight anymore. And she told them. Everything. All of it. From the push and pull of her marriage to the confrontation with her parents to Roderick's declaration of love less than an hour before. And though the ladies exchanged a few looks during the recitation of all the facts, they didn't interrupt.

"How can this be true?" Clarissa ended. "After everything, all that I settled myself in for the future. How can everything be turned on its head in this way?"

"That, my dear, is life," Esme said gently. "It's wonderful that way, in that the moment we think we understand something, it turns upside down and we start anew in seeing it."

"No, that sounds horrid," Clarissa said with a shake of her head.

"Only because the changes in the past sound like they have been awful," Marianne said. "And so change becomes fearful. Honestly, though, the question of how his heart changed and his feelings matters very little in this scenario. What matters more to me is you. How do *you* feel about him?"

Clarissa blinked. That was the question she had tried to ignore from the first moment she met him. When she'd seen him as an enemy, as an interloper determined to ruin everything out of self-ishness.

That had changed, of course, but she had kept him at arm's length regardless. She'd reminded herself, every time she felt a flutter of something beyond desire or passion or friendship, that he was not hers. She had never let her mind label herself as his, even when he demanded she claim that position in his bed.

Now she shut her eyes and Roderick's face danced easily before her. She smiled despite herself, feeling all the small and big ways he'd ever taken care of her. She thought of his kindness and his generosity. She thought of how he warmed a room when he entered, drawing all who met him closer, including her, even when she didn't want that.

She thought of how he took care of her. Tended to her physical needs, yes, but more than that. He watched and guarded her heart. He championed her to anyone who threatened her.

Even herself.

"You love him," Esme said softly.

Clarissa opened her eyes. "How—how do you know?"

"I see it in every bit of you," Esme said. "I feel it coming off of you in waves. And I understand the fight against it. The belief that it couldn't be because of…" She frowned. "Because of things out of your control. Actions that were taken that weren't your own, but have plotted the course of your life so far."

Clarissa nodded. "Yes."

"You want to run because it's so much to look at someone so magical and wonderful and know that he would fold you into himself and love you for all you are. Even the parts you don't yet love yourself. It feels too much."

"Yes." Clarissa felt herself crying again. She didn't even try to stop it.

"It is too much," Esme said, and then she smiled and she was so beautiful then. "It's too much and it's everything and it's worth the fear that makes it so hard to accept. Trust me, I know quite a bit about it."

"Oh, Esme," Marianne said with a gasping sob of her own. "I'm so happy you and Finn are happy and together. That you overcame everything. You both deserve the light you've brought to each other." She smiled at Clarissa. "And you deserve that too. It sounds like Kirkwood truly adores you. To reform a rake is very worth it. They do make the best husbands. Since he's already yours, since you do already love him and he declares he loves you, why throw away everything that could mean for you? And him? And your children?"

Children. It was impossible not to think of those imaginary children now. With Roderick's smile and her eyes. Impossible not to picture him becoming the kind and caring father he'd lost and wrapping their future family in the same love he now offered to gift her.

"It is better than you could ever dream, to be truly yourself with another person. To be loved in all your faces and expressions," Esme said.

Clarissa shivered. She'd spent so much time trying to be someone palatable. "The very idea is almost too much."

"Are you willing to take the risk?" Esme asked.

"He did. He did so bravely by declaring it tonight. And then letting me go, giving me the space to think about it." She dropped her head. "But it's different for us. A lady isn't meant to make these kinds of emotional decisions."

"Do you despise him for his grand emotions?" Marianne asked, her brow wrinkling.

"No," Clarissa said immediately. "When I see those emotions on his face, all I see is how beautiful he is."

"Yours are beautiful too," Esme said, and motioned to the mirror angled above the fireplace. "Look."

Clarissa set her cup down and moved to the mirror. She stared up at herself and drew in a breath. She almost glowed after talking about her love for Roderick. She'd never seen that on her face before.

She'd never felt it, either. But when she let it in, let it be there, it felt so right.

"I need to go to him. Gracious, I'm the rudest visitor, showing up, pouring all this out and running off into the night."

"I don't know," Esme said with a laugh as she stood. "It all seems very exciting to me. I do adore a good love story."

"So do I," Marianne said, rising to ring the bell. "I hope you'll let us know how it goes. And let us support you on this wonderful journey you're about to take."

"I will," Clarissa said, and smiled at them as the servant who arrived at the countess's call then ran off to have her carriage brought back. She didn't feel like she'd burdened them with her feelings at all. She felt closer to them for pouring a part of herself out. For allowing them to give something of equal value back. That was what Roderick meant when he said that just because something was proper it didn't mean it was right.

This felt right. Just as he felt right.

She stepped up into the carriage when it arrived and blew a kiss to her friends, who waved with excitement as she made her way back to Roderick. To the future she was about to grasp with both hands, if she could only find a way to fully surrender to it.

Roderick knew he had done the right thing by letting Clarissa go to give space to her feelings. She'd been so controlled for so long, the freedom was what she deserved. But he paced his study nearly two hours after she'd left and couldn't settle himself. All he could do was think of her shocked expression when he declared his heart.

There was a light knock on his door and he pivoted toward it. Stevenson stepped in. "Lady Kirkwood returned about half an hour ago, my lord."

"Half an hour!" Roderick burst out as he launched himself from the chair where he'd been brooding.

"Yes. She asked that I wait to tell you so she could ready a few things. Now she has requested that you join her in your chamber."

Roderick blinked aside the shock and took in the facts. Clarissa was back. Quite soon, too, when he took into account the travel time between Ramsbury's and his own home. What did that mean?

"My lord, are you well?" Stevenson asked with a concerned expression.

"I am," he declared, though he didn't know if it was true. "I am. My apologies. Thank you."

The butler appeared uncertain as he stepped from the room and Roderick took a moment to look at himself in the mirror. "You must allow her whatever time she needs with this. It's a war and there will be battles lost and won for her heart," he said.

The words didn't make him feel better.

He straightened his jacket and then stepped into the hall. He made his way upstairs to their chamber and stepped inside. The door to his room was closed, but hers was open and when he locked the door behind him, she called out to him. "Roderick, I'm in my chamber. Please join me."

His heart was pounding so hard, he wondered if she could hear it. He drew in a few ragged breaths as he stepped into her room. And then he stopped breathing at all. She stood at the foot of her bed and she was wearing the pink dress he'd chosen for her. He staggered at how beautiful she looked in color, how she shone as she smiled at him gently.

But she said nothing. She simply picked up her copy of *The Mirror of Graces* from its place on her side table. She walked around the bed to the fireplace and then turned. Never breaking her stare from his face, she tossed the book into the flames.

He rushed forward a step, watching with her as the tome slowly burned.

"Clarissa," he breathed.

She moved toward him. "I clung to those rules because I never thought I could be enough. But—but then I see myself in your eyes and that's who I am. Who I want to be." She moved closer. "Yours."

He nearly buckled. "Mine?"

She nodded slowly. "You told me earlier today that you loved me. The fact is that I-I love you too."

The way she stopped talking and her breath became shaky made it clear that this idea was as terrifying to her as it was to him. How he loved that they could support and navigate the unknown territory together. Together because she loved him.

"Could you truly love me?" she whispered. "It seems a dream."

"It *is* a dream," he said, and now he came to her, drawing her against him, loving the feel of her, the look of her as she stared up into his eyes with such adoration. Such love that she no longer hid. "But we're both awake. I love you with all I am, Clarissa. All I am and ever shall be."

"Good," she said, and lifted up toward him. "Then there is nothing in the world that could ever break us apart."

They kissed, their arms tightening around each other, their soft sighs of pleasure and love and surrender merging as they fell into her bed and into each other.

And all the lightning he'd ever desired struck all over again. It would strike every time he touched her, he realized. For as long as they both lived.

EPILOGUE

Roderick watched Clarissa across the room of their friends and family, his hand tightly gripping his glass of port. She was standing with her parents, as well as Lady Delacourt, but for once his wife seemed not to be troubled by whatever they were saying. The Lockharts had softened since their confrontation a few weeks ago. Roderick believed that had more to do with their desire to be financially supported than with any real emotion, but as long as they treated his wife well and it was what she wanted, he would let it stand.

"Are you planning on ripping my uncle and aunt to shreds?"

He turned and smiled as George stepped up. "If I said yes, would you call me out to protect the family honor?"

George chuckled. "The only family honor I care about in this room is Clarissa's. And you seem to be a good guardian of that. It seems from the way you look at her and she at you that your lightning struck after all."

"It did," he murmured as his wife met his eyes and a little pink entered her cheeks. Perhaps she was thinking of what he'd been doing to her in their chamber even as their guests arrived. What he intended to do to her again as soon as they departed.

"I'm glad. I might not believe in love, but I certainly am happy to see those I care about find it." George let out a little sigh.

"You might find it yet," Roderick suggested as he nudged his friend.

George glanced at him and there was a brief flash of sadness in his stare. "My mother has arranged a marriage. I've agreed. It's time, I think."

Roderick's lips parted. "George—"

"Don't trouble yourself," his friend said softly. "I never expected or wanted what you have. And I'll be happy."

Roderick wasn't certain of that, but he had no intention of getting into it with George at this moment. Not when Clarissa had extracted herself from the others and was coming across the room toward him.

George smiled. "I'll leave you to her and go keep my uncle and aunt busy."

He left Roderick's side and stopped as he and Clarissa met in the middle of the big parlor. He kissed her cheek and said something soft to her, something that made her smile up at her cousin. Then she continued to Roderick and when she reached him, all trouble was gone. It was only her.

"May a gentleman take his lady onto the terrace for some air?"

She nodded. "A lady would very much like that."

They exited onto the terrace and she slipped her arm through his as they walked to the edge and looked out over the pretty gardens, now dormant for the winter about to arrive.

"I think it's still pretty, even when it's in waiting," she said.

He smiled. "I agree. There's something special about the anticipation of all the beauty and joy and pleasure to come."

She glanced up at him and her lips tilted in a smile. "Are you talking about the garden or us?"

"The garden, of course," he said with a laugh. "You will never be in waiting when it comes to me. Though I very much anticipate when we're alone so I can kiss you."

She leaned into him, her arms coming around his neck as her gaze went soft and dreamy in the moonlight. "Why don't you be very inappropriate and kiss me now?"

"Why, Lady Kirkwood," he said with a chuckle. "Are you certain that would be prop—"

He didn't get to finish. Instead she leaned up and kissed him instead. Propriety be damned.

EXCERPT OF THE COURTESAN'S PROTECTOR

ABOUT AN EARL BOOK 3 (OUT APRIL 8, 2025)

"I think that's enough."

Jane jolted at the interruption from behind the viscountess. Both women turned toward it at the same time and heat filled Jane's cheeks as she realized it was Ripley who stood there, his handsome face impassive even if there was tension to every muscle in his body.

The viscountess glared at him. "And just who the hell are you to tell me such a thing?" Ripley tilted his head and said nothing, just stared at her, unspeaking and unmoving until she shifted. "Another one of the whore's lovers? Of course."

She pivoted and stomped across the room, raising her voice as she said, "Come along, Stuart, I think the quality of this shop has gone down significantly. I cannot imagine shopping here anymore."

The viscount looked confused at the sudden and very rude order, but he followed his wife out like a whipped dog, the ring of the bell echoing in Jane's ears as the door slammed behind them.

She rested her hands on the countertop and took a few breaths before she lifted her eyes back to Ripley. His tall, broad-shouldered beauty was a bit of a balm on her soul, even if she wished he hadn't been involved in this humiliation.

"That seemed personal," he said softly.

She shrugged. "An old lover."

His brows lifted. "And the wife was confronting you over it?"

"*She* was the lover," she said with a laugh. She had no concerns at Ripley's reaction to that revelation. Some might be shocked at the idea, but she knew his proclivities. They seemed to be of a mind that pleasure was pleasure and the source was not that important.

He nodded. "Ah, I see. And was the lady always so…pleasant?"

"Never quite so directly cruel, no," Jane said. "And her fire was much more endearing when it came with money to sooth it. I think it was a shock to her to see me here, twisted further into her world. I'm sure her husband doesn't know she takes female lovers, I'm certain she never told him she's never orgasmed with anyone but a woman." She sighed. "She has to strike before I do and I don't doubt Elizabeth will."

"You think she'd try to ruin you?" Ripley asked.

"She said she would. Right before she called me a whore and you so kindly interrupted like a knight to the rescue."

Ripley's mouth tightened. "Not a knight, I assure you. Just a concerned friend."

She stared at him a moment. Over the past few years, they *had* become what both of them would label friends. Esme had become a fighter in his stable and had bloomed, even before she found the love of her life and married, returning to the world where she belonged. Jane had struggled at being so near the man before her, but she'd found ways to do it. To cherish what he was and not hope for what he could have been if it was a different world or a different life.

But there were times, like now, when he stood close to her and she could see the fascinating bend of his nose up close, the slash of his scar across his eyebrow, the harsh line of his clean-shaven jaw, the dark promise of his brown eyes and she longed to fall into him.

Only once she started falling for a man like this, there wouldn't be an end to it. She would fall forever and that was terrifying.

"I'm happy to have such a friend," she said with false brightness. "But you cannot have come here today only to save me from dragons dressed in diamonds. Were you here to shop my wares or for some other reason?"

He smiled a little, though it didn't reach his eyes. "Actually, I've come on an errand from mutual friends. Delacourt was at the boxing club this morning and he brought a personal invitation to a fete he and Esme are hosting next week. He mentioned you hadn't responded yet and asked if I would check with you."

Jane bent her head. "Oh. Yes, the invitation. I received it a few days ago."

"But you haven't answered," he said evenly.

"No." She sighed. "It isn't that I don't want to see Esme. I miss her terribly. But…"

"But she's back in her world."

Jane nodded. "And if that encounter you interrupted tells me anything, it's a stark reminder that I don't belong anywhere near that world. I hardly belong in the one where I currently reside."

Her hands were still clenched on the countertop and Ripley reached out to cover one. He never wore gloves and so it was his bare skin that touched hers. She sucked in a breath as she lifted her gaze to his. There were only a few times where this man had ever touched her over the years and those fleeting grazes always stirred such things in her. Heated desires and dangerous hints of emotion.

"Esme loves you," he said.

Jane struggled to find her breath and her words. To break the spell of this moment somehow. At last she turned to frivolous flirtation, always a refuge with this man. She slipped her hand away from his and said, "I know. Everyone does."

He smiled a little at her playful response. "How could they not? Truly, Jane, do come. I'll need saving from the fops at the very least."

She arched a brow. "You? The Dragon needs saving from a bunch of ladies and gentlemen in frilly costume?"

"The Dragon isn't allowed to respond like he would in the ring," Ripley replied with a laugh.

She sighed. "For you and for her, I'll be there. I'll send word today."

"Good." He inclined his head slightly. "And now I must get back to my club before Brentwood allows them to have full brawls in the middle of the main ring."

She smiled at the mention of Ripley's right hand man. He was a serious sort, so the idea that he'd let those who trained there do anything wrong was laughable. "Oh yes, wouldn't want that to happen. Good day, Ripley."

He moved to the door and gave her a little bow. "See you soon, Janie."

Her heart fluttered at the endearment he sometimes used when he spoke to her. Fluttered as she watched him walk away from her, out her door, down the street through the shop windows. And though she would see him again in just a few scant days, she still felt the little ache that always tightened her heart whenever he walked away from her.

The one that she feared would bring her to her knees in the end, no matter how carefully she avoided that outcome.

Find The Courtesan's Protector at retailers everywhere on April 8, 2025!

The Broken Duke

The Silent Duke

The Duke of Nothing

The Undercover Duke

The Duke of Hearts

The Duke Who Lied

The Duke of Desire

The Last Duke

To see a complete listing of Jess Michaels' titles, please visit:

http://www.authorjessmichaels.com/books

ABOUT THE AUTHOR

USA Today Bestselling author Jess Michaels likes geeky stuff, Cherry Vanilla Coke Zero, anything coconut, cheese and her dog, Elton. She is lucky enough to be married to her favorite person in the world and lives in Oregon settled between the ocean and the mountains.

When she's not trying out new flavors of Greek yogurt or rewatching Bob's Burgers over and over and over (she's a Tina), she writes historical romances with smoking hot characters and emotional stories. She has written for numerous publishers and is now fully indie.

Jess loves to hear from fans! So please feel free to contact her at Jess@AuthorJessMichaels.com.

Jess Michaels offers a free book to members of her newsletter, so sign up on her website:
http://www.AuthorJessMichaels.com/

facebook.com/JessMichaelsBks
instagram.com/JessMichaelsBks
bookbub.com/authors/jess-michaels

www.ingramcontent.com/pod-product-compliance
Lightning Source LLC
Chambersburg PA
CBHW032220190726
48289CB00007BA/2314